"I Need A Husband," Desiree Said In A Breathless Voice.

Carter's head snapped back around. His icy blue eyes focused intently on her face.

"I'm willing to sign over half the Rimrock Ranch to you if you'll agree to marry me. Of course," she added hastily, "it would be a marriage in name only."

Desiree gripped his arm, as though she could hold him there until he responded in the way she wished him to answer. She chanced a look into his eyes and was surprised by the humor she saw there. His lips twisted in a mocking smile.

"Surely you could get a husband in a more conventional way, Miss Parrish," he replied.

Dear Reader,

Welcome to March and to Silhouette Desire! Our *Man of the Month, Wrangler's Lady,* is from an author many of you have told me is one of your favorites: Jackie Merritt. But this story isn't *just* a *Man of the Month,* it's also the first book in Jackie's exciting new series, THE SAXON BROTHERS.

Next: HAWK'S WAY *is back!* Joan Johnston continues her popular series with *The Cowboy Takes a Wife,* where we learn all about Faron Whitelaw's— from *The Cowboy and the Princess*—half brother, Carter Prescott.

The tie-ins and sequels just keep on coming, with Raye Morgan's *The Daddy Due Date*—a tie-in to last month's *Yesterday's Outlaw*—and BJ James's *The Hand of an Angel,* which continues her terrific books about the McLachlan brothers.

If you're looking for something completely different, you *must* pick up *Carolina on My Mind* by Anne Marie Winston. Here, our hero and heroine are abducted by aliens . . . and that's just for starters! And if you're looking for *humor,* don't miss *Midnight Ice* by Cathie Linz.

Miniseries and tie-ins, bold men and adventurous heroines, the supernatural and humor . . . there's something for *everyone* here at Silhouette Desire. So enjoy.

All the best,

Lucia Macro
Senior Editor

Please address questions and book requests to:
Reader Service
U.S.: P.O. Box 1325, Buffalo, NY 14269
Canadian: P.O. Box 1050, Niagara Falls, Ont. L2E 7G7

JOAN JOHNSTON
THE COWBOY TAKES A WIFE

SILHOUETTE *Desire*®
Published by Silhouette Books
America's Publisher of Contemporary Romance

SILHOUETTE BOOKS

ISBN 0-373-05842-X

THE COWBOY TAKES A WIFE

This edition published by arrangement with Harlequin Enterprises B. V.

® and TM are trademarks of Harlequin Enterprises B. V., used under
license. Trademarks indicated with ® are registered in the United States
Patent and Trademark Office, the Canadian Trade Marks Office and in
other countries.

Printed in U.S.A.

Books by Joan Johnston

Silhouette Desire

Fit To Be Tied #424
Marriage by the Book #489
Never Tease a Wolf #652
A Wolf in Sheep's Clothing #658
A Little Time in Texas #710
Honey and the Hired Hand #746
*The Rancher and the Runaway Bride #779
*The Cowboy and the Princess #785
*The Wrangler and the Rich Girl #791
*The Cowboy Takes a Wife #842

*Hawk's Way

JOAN JOHNSTON

started reading romances to escape the stress of being
an attorney with a major national law firm. She soon
discovered that writing romances was a lot more fun
than writing legal bond indentures. Since then, she has
published a number of historical and contemporary
category romances. In addition to being an author,
Joan is the mother of two children. In her spare time,
she enjoys sailing, horseback riding and camping.

For my friend and fellow trail rider,
Priscilla Kelly.
May we have many more long, lazy
rides through orange groves on the ridge.
Ride him, Cowgirl!
Giddyap Sadie!

One

Desiree Parrish had been secretly observing Carter Prescott throughout the Christmas pageant. So she saw the moment when his jaw tightened, when he closed his eyes and clenched his fists as though he were in pain. A bright sheen of tears glistened along his dark lashes. Moments later he rose from the back pew in which he sat and quietly, almost surreptitiously, left the church.

For a moment Desiree wasn't sure what to do. She didn't want to leave because her daughter, Nicole, hadn't yet performed her part as an angel in the pageant. Nicole *was* an angel, Desiree thought with a swell of maternal pride. But it was because of her five-year-old daughter that she needed Carter Prescott's help. Desiree had to speak privately with the cowboy, and she wasn't sure if she would get another opportunity like this one.

According to his grandmother, Madelyn Prescott, Carter had come to Wyoming from Texas looking for someplace to settle down. What if Carter moved on before she got a chance to make her offer to him? What if he decided to leave town tonight? Without giving herself more chance for thought, Desiree rose and headed for the nearest exit. She made a detour to grab her coat and wrap a scarf around her face to protect her from the frigid Wyoming weather.

Desiree was alarmed when she stepped outside to discover her quarry had disappeared into the night, hidden by the steady, gentle snowfall. She frantically searched the church parking lot, running through the fluffy snow in the direction his footprints led, afraid he would get away before she could make her proposition known to him.

She cried out in alarm when a tall, intimidating figure suddenly stepped from behind a pickup. She automatically put up a hand as though to ward off a blow. There was a moment of awful tension while she waited for the first lash of pain. In another instant she realized how foolish she had been.

She had found Carter Prescott. Or rather, he had found her.

"Are you all right?"

She heard the concern in his voice, yet when he reached out to touch her she took a reflexive step backward. It took all her courage to stand her ground. She had to get hold of herself. Her safety, and Nicole's, depended on what she did now.

Disconcerted by the growing scowl on Carter's face, she lowered her arm and threaded her fingers tightly together. "I'm fine," she murmured.

"Why did you follow me?" he demanded in a brusque voice.

"I..." Desiree couldn't get anything more past the sudden tightness in her throat. The cowboy looked sinister wrapped in a shearling coat with his Stetson pulled down low to keep out the bitter cold. He towered over her, and she had second thoughts about speaking her mind.

But she had no choice. It was two weeks until Christmas. She had to have a husband by the new year, and this cowboy from Texas was the most likely candidate she had found. She examined Carter closely in the stream of light glowing from the church steeple.

From the looks of his scuffed boots and ragged jeans, life hadn't been kind to him. His face was as weathered as the rest of him. He had wide-set, distrustful blue eyes and a hawkish nose. His jaw was shadowed with at least a day's growth of dark beard. His chin jutted—with arrogance or stubbornness, she wasn't sure which. From having seen it in church, she knew his hair was a rich, wavy chestnut brown. He had full lips, but right now they were flattened in irritation. Nonetheless, he was a handsome man. More good-looking than she deserved, everything considered.

"Look, lady, if you've got something to say, spit it out."

Desiree responded to the harsh voice with a shiver that she chose to blame on the cold. Plainly the cowboy wasn't going to stand there much longer. It was now or never.

Desiree spoke quickly, her breath creating a cloud of white around her. "My name is Desiree Parrish. I know from having spoken to your grandmother before the pageant this evening that you're looking for a place to set down some roots."

His scowl became a frown, but she hurried on without stopping. "I have a proposition to make to you."

She opened her mouth and then couldn't speak. What was she doing? Maybe this was only going to make things worse, not better. After all, what did she really know about Carter Prescott? The grown man standing before her was a stranger. She wondered whether he remembered the one time they had met. His eyes hadn't revealed whether he recognized her name when she had spoken it. But, maybe he had never known her name. After all, they had only spent fifteen minutes together twenty-three years ago, when she was a child of five and he was a lanky boy of ten.

It was spring, and Carter Prescott had come from King's Castle with his father to visit the Rimrock Ranch, since the two properties bordered each other. She would never even have met him if her kitten hadn't gotten stuck in a tree.

She had been trying to coax Boots down by talking to her, but the kitten had been afraid to move. The ten-year-old boy had heard Desiree's pleading cries and come to investigate. She thought now of all the reactions Carter could have had to the situation. He might have ignored her. Or come to see the problem but left her to solve it herself. He might have made fun of her or taunted her about the kitten's plight. After all, she was just a kid, and a girl at that.

Carter Prescott had done none of those things. He had patted her awkwardly on the shoulder and promised to get Boots down from the tree. He had climbed up into the willow and reached for the kitten. But Boots evaded his reach. He had finally lurched for the kitten and caught her, but cat and boy had come tumbling down in a heap on the ground.

Desiree had screamed in fright and hurried over to make sure Boots was all right. She found her kitten carefully cushioned in the boy's arms.

He had handed Boots to her with a grim smile. "Here's your cat."

She was too busy fussing over Boots to notice Carter's attempts to rise. It was his gasp of pain that caused her to look at him again. That was when she saw the bloody bone sticking out through his jeans above the knee.

Her second panicked scream brought their fathers on the run. Her father picked her up and hugged her tight, grateful she was all right. She babbled the problem out to him, her voice too hysterical at first for him to realize what had happened.

Carter's father bent down on one knee to his son. His lips had tightened ominously before he said, "Your mother will give me hell for this."

Carter hadn't made a sound when his father picked him up and carried him toward their pickup. His face had been white, his teeth clamped on his lips to stop any sound from escaping. Desiree had tried to follow him but her father had held her back.

"Let the boy be, Desiree," he'd said. "He won't want to cry in front of you."

"But Daddy, I have to see how he is," she protested. "He saved Boots."

Her father relented, and she ran after Carter and his father.

"I'm sorry," Desiree called up to Carter, her tiny legs rushing to keep pace.

"You ought to be," Carter's father said.

Stunned at the meanness in his voice, Desiree stopped in her tracks. But Carter turned to face her over his father's shoulder. He nodded and tried to smile, and she knew he had forgiven her.

But she and Carter had never crossed paths again. When she asked about him several days later, her father had told her that Carter had been visiting Wyoming for only a few days. His parents were divorced and Carter lived in Texas with his mother. He wouldn't be coming back.

Desiree had never seen Carter again, until he showed up at the Christmas pageant in Casper tonight. Was she willing to gamble her future on a man she had known for barely fifteen minutes twenty-three years ago? It seemed idiotic in the extreme.

Desiree wasn't an idiot. But she was in urgent need of a husband. Carter might not be the same person now as he had been then. But she remembered vividly how he had cradled the kitten to keep it from harm at the expense of his own welfare. Surely he could not have grown up a cruel man. She was staking her life on it.

Carter was already turning to walk away, when she laid a slender hand on his arm. She tensed when she felt the steely muscle tighten even through the sheepskin coat.

"I need a husband," she said in a breathless voice.

Carter's head snapped back around. His icy blue eyes focused intently on her face.

"I'm willing to sign over half the Rimrock Ranch to you if you'll agree to marry me. Of course," she added hastily, "it would be a marriage in name only."

His eyes narrowed, and she found herself racing to get everything out before she lost her nerve. "The Rimrock is the second largest outfit in the area, nearly as big as King's Castle, your father's place. It's got good water and lots of grass. The house was built by my great-great-grandfather. You'd be getting a good bargain. What do you say?''

Desiree gripped his arm tighter, as though she could hold him there until he responded in the way she wished him to answer. She chanced a look into his eyes and was surprised by the humor she saw there. His lips twisted in a mocking smile.

''Surely you could get a husband in a little more conventional way, Miss Parrish,'' he replied.

This wasn't a laughing matter. The sooner Carter Prescott realized that, the better. Desiree reached up and pulled aside the heavy wool scarf that was wrapped around her face.

''You're mistaken, Mr. Prescott.'' She angled her face so he could see the vivid scar that slanted across her right cheek from chin to temple. ''No man would willingly choose me for a bride.''

She raised wary brown eyes to the man before her and shuddered at the cold, hard look on his face. Her shoulders slumped. She should have known better. She should have known even the promise of the Rimrock wasn't enough to entice a man to face her over the breakfast table for the rest of his life.

Desiree hurriedly wrapped the scarf back around her face to hide the scar. ''This was a stupid idea,'' she muttered. ''Forget I mentioned it.''

Desiree quickly stumbled away, embarrassed by the stinging tears that had sprung to her eyes. It would have been humiliating enough to have him refuse her offer. She didn't want him to see how devastated she was by his reaction to the scar on her face. It had been so long since she had exposed herself to someone for the first time that she had forgotten the inevitable horror it caused.

She would have to find another way to save herself. But merciful Lord in heaven, what was she going to do?

Meanwhile, Carter had been so stunned by the entire incident that Desiree had nearly reached the door of the church before he recovered himself enough to speak. By then he was glad she was gone, because he wouldn't have known what to say. He stared after her, remembering the look of vulnerability in her deep brown eyes when she had exposed her face.

He was amazed even now at the strength of his reaction to the awful sight he had seen. He had felt fury at the destruction of something that had obviously once been quite beautiful. And pity for what it must be like to live with such a scar. And disgust that she had been reduced to begging for a spouse.

If he was honest, he also had to admit that his curiosity was piqued. How had she been wounded so horribly? Why was she so anxious to find a husband? And why had she singled him out?

Carter wondered if she remembered the one time they had met. It was a day he had never forgotten. He unconsciously rubbed his thigh. His thigh bone—

the one he had broken saving her blasted cat—still ached when the weather was wet or cold. If he got tired enough, he sometimes limped. He never had liked cats much since.

For other reasons that day was etched in his memory like brutally carved glass. The scene between his mother and father when his mom had arrived at the emergency room of the hospital had been loud and vicious. It was easy to see why his parents hadn't stayed married. They had been in the process of a divorce when he was conceived, and he had been born before the divorce was final. His mother just hadn't seen fit to inform his father of that fact. She had only brought him to Wyoming to meet his father because Wayne Prescott had accidentally found out about his son and demanded visitation rights.

The incident at the Rimrock Ranch had convinced his mother that his father was not a fit custodian. That day had been the first and last he had seen of Wayne Prescott. So Carter remembered well his first meeting with Desiree Parrish. It had been a dark day in his life.

Desiree was correct in her assumption that he wanted roots, but his wants and needs had culminated in a specific objective. He wanted the land that would have been his inheritance if his mother and father hadn't divorced. He wanted King's Castle.

Unfortunately, on his father's death the land had gone in equal shares to his father's very young widow, Belinda Prescott, and his father's bastard son, Faron Whitelaw. Carter had already made a generous offer to them for the land. They had promised him an answer tonight.

He felt queasy at the thought that they might refuse him. Where would he go if he couldn't stay at King's Castle? Where would he find the solace he so desperately needed from the memories that relentlessly trailed him wherever he went? He had been running for so long—six years—that he had begun to wonder if there would ever be an end to it.

As he stepped into the cab of his pickup and headed back to King's Castle, he couldn't help thinking about the offer Desiree Parrish had made to him. He remembered well the lush, grassy valleys to be found on the Rimrock. A river carved its way over the prairie, right through the ranch. The ranch house was a two-story, wooden-planked structure, simple but enduring. He had never seen the inside.

To tell the truth, before he had discovered King's Castle was on the market, he had inquired about purchasing the Rimrock. His agent had been told, in no uncertain terms, that the ranch was not for sale. So why had Desiree Parrish offered him half the place for his name on a marriage certificate? And how could she have believed that someone rich enough to buy the Rimrock, lock, stock and barrel, would bargain away his freedom for it?

Unless she doesn't know you're rich.

Carter found himself chuckling as he realized the image he must have presented to the young woman, unshaven, with his jeans frayed and his boots worn to a nub. Apparently his grandmother hadn't told Desiree his true circumstances. He sobered abruptly. He had learned, to his sorrow, that wealth couldn't buy happiness. In fact, it had been the source of great tragedy in his life.

Carter felt the tension pounding behind his eyes. He never should have given in to his grandmother's pleas for him to attend the Christmas pageant. Tonight the memories had come back to haunt him. Listening to those childish voices, seeing those angelic faces, had brought all the pain of betrayal and loss back into sharp focus. He wanted to forget the past, but he wasn't sure it was possible. Guilt rode heavy on his shoulders. And regret. And anger.

Carter stopped his truck in front of the ranch house at King's Castle, a three-story stone structure with turrets and crenels, which his father had called The Castle. It didn't fit this land anywhere near as well as the simple house on the Rimrock. He headed around back to the kitchen door, which he knew would be open. He found his way through the darkened house to the elegant parlor, where a fire still glowed in the grate. He stirred the ashes and added a log from the pile nearby. Finally, he poured himself a whiskey and settled into the chair near the fireplace, where he could empty his mind of the painful past and concentrate on the future.

It was Desiree Parrish who filled his thoughts. He remembered how tiny, almost delicate, she had seemed next to his great size, how the snowflakes had gathered on her dark hair and eyelashes. Those memories were overshadowed by the look of fear in her huge brown eyes when she had revealed her scar to him. And by the way she had braced herself for his revulsion.

It was true the scar was ugly, but Carter had shifted his gaze to her eyes, which had called out to him. He had seen a wounded spirit that was the equal of his own. It had taken a great deal of effort to resist reaching out to fold her protectively in his arms. Fortunately, she had run before he could do something so foolishly impulsive.

Carter didn't know how long he had been sitting there, when he heard Madelyn and Belinda Prescott and Faron Whitelaw returning. He felt his gut tighten, reminding him how much their answer mattered to him. He wanted this place; he *needed* this place, if he was ever to forget the past and go on with his life.

Madelyn entered the room scolding. "What happened to you, young man? There were several more people I wanted you to meet, although I suppose we can have a party here and—"

He had risen the instant she came into the room and was already there to help her out of her coat. "I'm not much interested in parties, Maddy."

"You should be," she countered. "Why, a handsome young man like you ought to be settled down now, with babies and—"

"I just want an answer from Belinda and Faron, one way or the other," he said sharply, cutting her off again. He laid her coat across the sofa, which gave him a chance to focus his attention anywhere except on Belinda and Faron. He was afraid he might see their answer to his offer on their faces. He was afraid that answer would be no.

At last, he forced himself to look at them. They were staring at each other, and he could feel the tension between them. His heart began to pound, sending blood rushing to his head, making him feel dizzy. He reached for his whiskey and swallowed a restoring gulp. He met his half brother's eyes and said, "Well, what have you decided?"

"Give us another few minutes," Faron said. "Belinda and I have some things we need to discuss before we can give you an answer." Faron quickly ushered Belinda out of the room and into the ranch office across the hall.

Carter crossed to the bar so he would have his back to his grandmother. He didn't want her to see the frustration—and fear—he felt. He poured a glass of port and turned to hand it to Madelyn. His casual calm was hard won. The hell of it was, he didn't think he was fooling Madelyn for a minute.

His grandmother settled herself on the sofa. Instead of launching into a thousand questions, she sipped her port and stared into the fire.

He was too nervous to sit and too proud to let Madelyn see him pacing anxiously. He hooked an arm over the mantel and focused on the map of King's Castle that hung above it. The boundaries had changed over the hundred-odd years the land had been owned by Prescotts, but even now it was an impressive spread. He froze when he heard the office door open.

"Maddy, can you come in here for a minute?" Faron called.

"Excuse me, Carter," the old woman said. "I hate to leave you alone. I'm sure I won't be gone long."

He didn't look at her, afraid that his feelings were naked on his face. "Don't worry, Maddy. I'm used to being alone."

He could have bitten his tongue after he'd said the words, knowing how much he had revealed in that simple sentence. He felt more than saw, her hesitation. But he heard her set her glass down on the end table and leave the room.

He shook his head in disgust. How had he let possessing The Castle matter so much to him? He was only setting himself up for disappointment. He should have come sooner, when Wayne Prescott was still alive, and demanded his heritage. But he hadn't needed Wayne's land then. He hadn't yet experienced the tragedy that had left him rootless and alone.

"Carter?"

Two

Desiree concentrated on the road, which was slick with a layer of ice and difficult to see through the blowing snow. She had been among the last to leave the church, since she had helped with the cleanup. The storm had worsened in the past hour, and Desiree wished she had asked someone to follow her, at least until she got to the turnoff for the ranch. She didn't want to end up stuck on the road somewhere overnight, although if she ended up frozen to death that would solve the worry of finding a husband.

Beside her, Nicole chattered on happily about the Christmas pageant. Desiree responded to her daughter, but her thoughts were elsewhere. She was mentally kicking herself for being so foolish as to confront a perfect stranger with a proposal of marriage.

"Did you see me, Mommy? Was I a good angel?"

"You were wonderful, sweetheart. A perfect angel."

Desiree worried her lower lip with her teeth. Why hadn't she stood firm until she had an answer from Carter Prescott? Because she was afraid, that's why! But although the ragtag cowboy's eyes had been cold, they hadn't been unkind. And while he had towered over her, she hadn't felt threatened. It had been the fear of rejection, not the fear of physical harm, that had sent her fleeing into the night.

"Did you see me fly, Mommy?"

Desiree smiled at the image of her daughter flapping her angel's wings. "I certainly did." She had watched the finish of the Christmas pageant from the shadows along the side aisle of the church, her chest aching with love—and fear. She *must* find a husband before the new year. Her safety, and Nicole's, depended on having a man's presence in the house. If only she had been less fainthearted about confronting Carter Prescott!

"Look at me, Mommy. Look! I can fly even without my wings!"

"Nicole! Sit down, and put your seat belt back on this instant!"

Nicole quickly dropped down on the seat and began hunting for the end of the seatbelt in the darkened cab.

Desiree had taken her eyes off the road only for a second, but that was enough. She caught a patch of ice and felt the pickup begin to slide. She turned the wheel into the skid and resisted the urge to brake, knowing that would only make things worse. But she could already see the truck wasn't going to recover in time to stay on the road.

Nicole gave a cry of alarm as the pickup began to tilt. "Mommy! We're falling!"

"It's all right, Nicole. Sit still. Everything will be fine." Desiree's heart pounded as the pickup slid sideways off the road into a shallow gully.

The truck thumped to a stop at a sharp angle with the right wheels lodged in snow two feet deeper than the left ones. It took a second for Desiree to realize they really were all right. Nicole whimpered in fright.

Desiree reached over and grabbed Nicole and pulled her daughter into her lap, hugging her tight. "It's all right, sweetheart. We're fine. Everything's fine."

"We're going to fall, Mommy."

"No, we're not. The truck is stopped now. It's wedged in the snow. It won't tip any more." But she wasn't going to be able to drive out of this gulley. Which meant that unless she wanted to spend the night in the truck, she was going to have to walk back the two miles or so to the church and call for help.

"You'll have to wait here for me, Nicole, while I—"

"No, Mommy! Don't leave me! I'm scared!"

Despite her daughter's cries, Desiree shifted her onto the seat. "I won't be gone long."

"Don't leave! Please, Mommy." Nicole clambered back into Desiree's lap and twined her arms around her mother's neck.

Desiree hugged her daughter, fighting the tears that stung her nose and welled in her eyes.

She had been on her own for six years. She had gone through her pregnancy alone and had raised Nicole without help from anyone. Forced to cope with whatever life had thrown at her, somehow she had survived. She and Nicole were a family. Sliding off the road wasn't nearly the disaster that loomed on the horizon. Soon their very lives would be in danger.

So what if she was stuck miles from home in the middle of a snowstorm with her daughter clinging to her neck like a limpet? They, and the truck, had endured without a scratch. There was no reason to cry. But her throat had swollen so thick it hurt to swallow, and she could feel the heat of a tear on her cold cheek.

It wasn't the accident that was causing her distress, she conceded; it was the knowledge that she had so little control over her life.

Desiree took a deep breath and let it out. She had managed so far to keep things together. She just had to take one step at a time. She retrieved the blanket she kept in the well behind the seat and wrapped Nicole snugly in it.

"Mommy has to call a tow truck to haul us out of here," she explained to Nicole. "The closest phone is at the church. You need to wait right here for me until I get back. Don't leave the truck. If you wander off, you could get lost in all this snow. Okay, sweetheart?"

It was a sign of how much more quickly the child of a single parent had to grow up that Nicole sniffed back her tears and nodded reluctant agreement to her mother's order. There was a risk leaving Nicole alone, but there was even greater risk in taking her out walking in the bitter cold.

"I won't be gone long," Desiree promised as she closed the truck door behind her. Desiree wished she had a warmer coat to keep out the bitter wind, but at least she had warm boots. She would be cold when she arrived at the church, but anyone who lived in Wyoming was inured to the harsh weather.

To Desiree's amazement, she had been walking no more than two minutes, when she saw headlights through the snow. She was afraid she would be lost in the dark at the side of the road, so she stepped out onto the pavement and waved her arms. She knew the moment when the driver spotted her, because the pickup did a little slide to the side as it slowed.

As soon as the truck stopped, she raced to the driver's window. The door had already opened, and a tall man was stepping out.

"I need help! I—"

"What the hell are you doing out here walking on a night like this? Where's your car?"

Desiree felt her heart thump when she realized she was staring into the furious eyes of Carter Prescott. "My truck slid into a ditch. I was going back to the church to call for a tow. Can you give me a ride?"

"Get in," he said curtly.

Desiree raced around to the other side of the pickup before Carter could reach out to touch her.

As he pulled his door closed he said, "It's doubtful you'll get a tow truck to come out in this storm. I'll give you a ride home."

Desiree debated the wisdom of arguing with him. But she would rather have Nicole safe and warm at home than have to wait with her daughter in the cold until a tow truck arrived. "All right. But I left something in my truck that I need to pick up. It's only a little way ahead."

When Carter pulled up behind her truck he said, "Do you need any help?"

"I can handle it." Desiree was struggling with the door on Nicole's side of the truck, when it was pulled open from behind her. She whirled in fright—to find Carter standing right behind her.

"I figured you could use some help, after all."

Desiree took a deep breath. This man wasn't going to harm her. She had to stop acting so jumpy around him. "Thank you," she said.

The instant the truck door opened, Nicole came flying out. Desiree barely managed to catch her before she fell. In fact, she would have fallen if Carter hadn't put his arms around Desiree and supported both her and the child.

"This is the something you needed to pick up?" he asked.

Desiree heard the displeasure underlying his amazement and responded defensively, "This is my daughter, Nicole."

"You didn't say anything about a kid earlier this evening."

"It wasn't necessary that you know about her until we had reached some agreement."

"I don't think—"

Desiree cut him off. "I would rather not discuss this further until we're alone." Which was tantamount to a suggestion that they ought to have further discussion on the matter in private, Desiree realized too late.

"All right," he said.

"You can let go now. I've got her."

He was slow to remove his support, and Desiree was aware suddenly of how secure she had felt with his arms around her. And of being very much alone without them.

She carried Nicole the short distance to his truck. He held the passenger door open, but she found it awkward to step up into the truck with Nicole in her arms.

"Give her to me," Carter's tone of voice made it plain he would rather not have handled the child. Before either Desiree or Nicole could protest, he had the girl in his arms.

Desiree had barely settled herself in the truck when Carter dropped Nicole on her lap, shoved her thin wool coat inside and slammed the truck door closed.

"The turnoff for the Rimrock is about five miles ahead on the right," Desiree instructed.

"I know."

"How—"

"I drove by there on the way to my grandmother's. I haven't forgotten visiting your place when I was ten."

She watched him rub his thigh and wondered about the bone he had broken so many years ago. "Does it still bother you?"

"Sometimes."

"I'm sorry."

"No need to be. It was my own fault."

He looked sinister in the green light reflected off the dash, not at all like the savior she had sought out in the parking lot of the church.

"What's your name?" Nicole asked. "Do you know my mommy? I was an angel tonight. Do you want to see me fly?"

Carter's lips flattened in annoyance.

In the uncomfortable silence that followed her daughter's questions, a frown grew in the space between Desiree's brows. Carter's refusal to answer Nicole was rude—or at least, inconsiderate. Did Carter simply not like children? Or was it just Nicole's behavior he didn't approve of?

Carter's lack of response did nothing to curb Nicole's curiosity.

"Are you coming to our house?"

"Yes," Carter replied sharply.

Desiree realized he had probably been curt in hopes of shutting her daughter up. But Nicole wasn't deterred by Carter's antagonism. The little girl had learned through dealing with a mother who was putty in her hands that persistence often won her what she wanted.

"Do you want to see my room?"

Carter sighed.

Desiree could see that he wanted to say no. He sought out her eyes, his lips pursed in displeasure. She decided to rescue him from her daughter's clutches.

"It's nearly bedtime, sweetheart. You'll have to wait to show Mr. Prescott your room until some other time." It was all she could do to keep her own displeasure at the cowboy's surliness out of her voice.

"Are you going to be my daddy?"

"Nicole!"

Desiree was mortified at the question because she had, in fact, proposed to the man sitting across from her, and because she hadn't realized Nicole was even aware that she was seeking a husband. The little girl's next words made it clear that she had thought of the idea all on her own.

"My friend Shirley has a daddy, but I don't. I asked Santa Claus for a daddy, but so far I haven't got one. Are you the daddy I asked for?"

"No," he said in a strangled voice.

"Oh. Well, it's not Christmas yet," Nicole said cheerfully. "Maybe Santa Claus will bring me a daddy."

Desiree was chagrined at her daughter's outspokenness. However, if she had anything to say about it, Nicole would get her wish, although Carter's attitude toward Nicole was a matter that needed further exploration before their discussion of marriage continued.

Carter was pleased when they reached the Rimrock ranch house to discover it was just as he remembered it. The two-story frame structure had been built to last by people who cared. Someone had planted pines and spruce around the house, and with the drifting snow it was a scene worthy of a picture postcard.

"Follow the road around to the back," Desiree said.

Carter didn't volunteer to carry Nicole from the truck, and Desiree didn't ask. But halfway to the door, and though it made his stomach clench, he took the little girl in his arms to relieve Desiree of a burden that was obviously too heavy for her.

To his surprise, when he reached for the doorknob, he discovered that Desiree had locked the back door. Most ranches, even in this day and age, were left open, a vestige of range hospitality from a time when homesteads had been few and far between.

"Afraid of the bogeyman?" he asked with a wry grin.

Desiree didn't smile back. "I have to think of Nicole's safety." She stepped inside, turned on the light and held the door for him.

Carter immediately set the little girl down. His heart thudded painfully as he watched her race gleefully across the room, headed for the hall. She turned on the light and kept going. Carter could hear her running up the stairs.

"Make yourself comfortable while I put her to bed," Desiree said, following Nicole down the hallway that led to the rest of the house. "We'll talk as soon as I get her down. There's coffee on the stove or brandy in the living room. Help yourself." Then she was gone.

Carter hadn't been in the house before, but he knew the moment he crossed the threshold that this was a home. A band tightened around his chest, making it hard to breathe. This was what he had been seeking. There was warmth and comfort here, not only for the body, but also for the soul.

The kitchen was cluttered, but clean. There were crayon drawings taped to the refrigerator, and a crock full of wooden spoons and a stack of cookbooks sat on an oak chest in the corner. The red-and-white linoleum floor was worn down to black in front of the sink, and the wooden round-leg table and ladderback chairs were scarred antiques. An old-fashioned tin coffeepot sat on the stove. Carter decided he would rather have the brandy.

He followed where Desiree had gone, down a hallway, past a formal dining room, to a combination office and parlor, where a stone fireplace took up one wall and a large rolltop desk took up most of another. A picture window took up the third wall. The fire had burned down to glowing embers, and Carter took the poker and stirred the ashes before adding another log.

A spruce Christmas tree stood in the corner, decorated with handmade ornaments. Above the fireplace, a set of longhorn steer horns a good six feet from tip to tip had been mounted.

Carter looked longingly at an old sofa and chairs that invited him to sit down. He heard a *whoosh* from the vents as the furnace engaged. As he surveyed the room, he realized that the aged quality he had admired so much in the furniture was as much the result of poverty as posterity. Certainly there were heirlooms here. But there was a shabbiness to the furnishings that could only be the result of limited funds.

Carter felt sick to his stomach. Maybe Desiree Parrish knew more about him than he had thought. Maybe she had come after him because she knew he had the money to restore this ranch to its former glory. He had been married once for his money. It wasn't an experience he intended to repeat.

He spied the wet bar where he found the brandy and glasses. "Would you like me to pour one for you?" he called up the stairs.

"Please. I'll join you in a moment," Desiree called down to him.

Desiree took a deep breath and let it out. She had another chance to persuade Carter Prescott that he should marry her. She had to do everything in her power to convince him that she—and the Rimrock—were a bargain he couldn't refuse.

She leaned over and kissed Nicole good night. "Sleep tight, sweetheart." She left a small night-light burning. Not for Nicole. It was Desiree who feared the dark. She had made it a habit to leave a light so she could check on her daughter without the rush of terror that always caught her unaware when she entered a dark room.

Desiree closed her daughter's bedroom door behind her and hurried across the hall to her own room. She slipped out of her coat, which she hadn't even realized she was still wearing. But she had turned the heat down before she'd left for church to conserve energy, and it took time for the furnace to take the frost out of the air.

She crossed to the old oak dresser with the gold-framed mirror above it and checked her appearance. This was a heaven-sent second opportunity, and she wanted to look her best. It had become a habit to sit at an angle before the dresser, so only the good side of her face was reflected back to her. She forced herself to face forward, to see what Carter Prescott would see.

There was no way to disguise the scar. It was a white slash that ran from chin to temple on her right side. Plastic surgery would have corrected it, but she didn't have the money for what would be purely cosmetic work. She put another layer of mascara on her lashes and freshened her lipstick. And she let her hair down. It was the one vanity she had left. It spread like rich brown silk across her shoulders and down to her waist.

She smoothed her black knit dress across a body that was curved in all the right places, but which she knew had brought her husband no pleasure. Desiree forced her thoughts away from the sadness that threatened to overwhelm her whenever she looked at herself in a mirror. She had to focus on the future, not the past. This was her last chance to make a good impression on Carter Prescott. She couldn't afford to waste it.

But it took all her courage to open the bedroom door and walk down the stairs.

Carter controlled the impulse to gasp as Desiree entered the parlor. It was the first time he had seen her when she wasn't shrouded in that moth-eaten coat. She moved with grace, her body slim and supple. Her dress hugged her body, revealing curves that most women would have died for. His groin tightened with desire.

He thought maybe his hands could almost span her waist. There wasn't much bosom, but more than a handful was a waste. His blood quickened at the thought that if she were his wife, he would have the right to hold her, to touch her, to seek out the secrets of her body and make them his.

He wasn't aware he was avoiding her face until he finally looked at it. His eyes dropped immediately to the brandy in his hands. He forced himself to look again, but focused on her eyes. They were a rich, warm brown, with long lashes and finely arched brows. It was clear she had once been a very beautiful woman. Once, but no more. The scar ran through her mouth on one side, twisting it down slightly.

"Did you pour a brandy for me?" she asked.

Carter realized he was staring and flushed. He welcomed the excuse to turn away, and shook his head slightly, aware he ought to do a better job of hiding his feelings. She had to look at that scar every day. The least he could do was face her without showing the pity he felt. He turned back to her with the drink in his hand and realized she had turned herself in profile, so he only saw the good side of her face. Desire stabbed him again.

He wondered if she had done it on purpose or whether it was an unconscious device she used to protect herself when she was with other people. At any rate, he was grateful for the respite that allowed him to speak to her without having to guard his expression.

Desiree took the drink from him. "Why don't you sit down and make yourself comfortable?" She gestured to a chair near the fire and sat down across from him on the sofa so he saw only her good side. "I never gave you a chance earlier this evening to respond to my proposal."

"I was glad for the time to think about what you had to say." Carter took a sip of his brandy.

"And?" Desiree held her breath, determined to wait for his answer. Her nerves got the better of her. She couldn't help making one last pitch. "You can see the house is comfortable." She forced a smile. "And I'm a good cook."

"Tell me again why you want to get married," he said in a quiet voice.

Desiree debated the wisdom of telling Carter the real reason she needed a husband. She had always believed honesty was the best policy. When she opened her mouth to speak, what came out was, "I've been on my own for six years. Nicole needs a father. I . . . the winters are long when you're alone.

And I could use a partner to help me do the heavy work on the ranch.

"As you've seen for yourself, my face makes it impossible for me to attract a husband in the conventional way. I decided to take matters into my own hands."

"Why me?"

"Your grandmother speaks highly of you." She smiled. "And I haven't forgotten how you saved Boots."

"Boots?"

"My cat."

He rubbed his thigh and grimaced. "Right."

So maybe she didn't know about his money, Carter thought. She wanted company. And a father for her child. And someone to do the heavy work on the ranch. That made sense. And he could understand why she didn't trust a man to see beyond the scar on her face. He was having trouble doing that himself, although his body had responded—was responding even now—to the thought of joining hers in bed. She had beautiful eyes. In profile, the scar didn't show at all. And in the dark...

He would be giving her something in return for something he wanted very badly. Carter knew he could put down roots here. This place felt like a real home. He wanted to make it his. Though Desiree apparently didn't know it, he had the money to restore the Rimrock to what it had once been, to make it even better.

He wanted to ask her when and where she had gotten the scar on her face, but he figured that could wait until they got to know each other better. Assuming they did.

"I have two problems with your proposal," he said.

Desiree had been certain he was going to say a flat no, so she welcomed the opportunity to overcome his objections. "What problems?"

Carter's lips thinned. "I hadn't counted on the girl. I'd want her kept out of my way."

Desiree bristled. "This is Nicole's home. I wouldn't think of confining her to any part of it to keep your paths from crossing. If you can't handle the fact that I have a daughter, this isn't going to work."

Carter was amazed at how Desiree's eyes flashed like fire when she was angry. In that moment, her scar made her look like a fierce warrior. He nodded abruptly. "All right." He supposed it wasn't necessary for her to keep the child out of his way; he would do whatever was necessary to keep his distance from the little girl.

"And the second problem?" Desiree asked.

"I can't agree to a marriage in name only."

Desiree paled. Her heart pounded, and her stomach rolled over so she felt like throwing up. She couldn't couple with any man, ever again. "Why not?" She forced out the words through stiff lips.

"I don't plan to spend the rest of my life as a monk. I'd expect my wife to provide the necessary comfort on cold winter nights."

Desiree flushed as his eyes boldly assessed her body. She found the man she had selected to be her husband quite handsome. But she had learned from bitter experience that a man became a beast when satisfying his sexual needs. She dreaded what he might expect of her. She was certain she had nothing to offer him.

But it would humiliate her to have her husband going to some other woman for his needs. In their small ranch community the talk would be bad enough if he married her. She didn't want to give her neighbors any more reason to gossip.

"I'm willing to compromise," she said at last.

"There is no compromise on this," he said. "Either you're willing to be my wife or you're not."

"I'm willing to be a real wife," she assured him. "But not until we know each other better."

Carter's lips twisted. "How long do you expect that to take?"

"I don't know." Desiree looked him in the eye and

Three

———

They decided to be married a week later in a civil ceremony in Casper. Desiree offered Carter the guest bedroom, but he decided to stay in a hotel in town until the wedding so he could take care of some unfinished business.

"I'd like Nicole to be present at the wedding," Desiree said as she stood holding his shearling coat for him at the kitchen door.

"Is that really necessary?"

"Once we're married, you'll be her father. I think it would help her to adjust better if she saw us take our vows."

"From what I've heard, she'll probably think I'm a gift from Santa Claus," he muttered.

Desiree couldn't help smiling. Chances were, Nicole would.

The day of the wedding dawned clear and crisp. Most of the snow had blown away or into drifts, revealing a vast expanse of golden grass. Desiree woke with a feeling of trepidation. Was marriage the right solution to her problem? Would she and Nicole achieve safety by bringing Carter Prescott into the house? Was that alone enough? She considered buying a gun to protect them, but realized that she wouldn't be able to use it, so it would only become one more danger.

Desiree was still snuggled under the warm covers when she heard the patter of bare feet on the hardwood floor. Her door opened and Nicole came trotting over to the four-poster.

"Where are your slippers, young lady?" Desiree chastised as she hauled Nicole up and under the covers with her.

Nicole promptly put her icy feet on Desiree's thigh.

"Your feet are freezing!"

Nicole giggled.

Desiree took her daughter's feet in her hands and rubbed them to warm them up. "Today's the day Mr. Carter and I are getting married," she reminded Nicole.

"Is he going to be my daddy now?"

"Uh-huh." Desiree hadn't asked how Carter felt about being called Daddy. Surely he wouldn't mind. After all, being called Daddy didn't require any effort on his part.

One of her major concerns over the past week had been how well Carter would get along with Nicole. During his visits he was brusque if forced to speak at all, but mostly he held himself aloof from Nicole. She supposed that was only natural for a man who apparently hadn't spent time around children. And a man his age—he must be thirty-three or thirty-four—probably didn't remember what it was like to be a child. Obviously he would need a little time to adjust.

Desiree glanced at the clock and realized that by the time she put a roast in the oven for their post-wedding dinner, she would barely have enough time to dress herself and Nicole and get into Casper before they were due in the judge's chambers. "We'd better get moving, or we're going to be late."

Desiree took a deep breath and let it out. For better or worse, her decision had been made. Whatever price she had to pay for her own and her daughter's safety was worth it. Marriage, even the duty of the marriage bed, was not too great a sacrifice.

Carter was having second thoughts of his own. He paced the empty hallway of the courthouse in Casper, waiting for his bride. The sound of his boot-steps on the marble floors echoed off the high ceilings. The loneliness of the years he had spent wandering kept him from bolting. *Roots*. Finally he had found a place where he could belong. He would settle down on the Rimrock and be a husband and father. Again.

He paused in midstep. The sudden tightness in his chest, the breathlessness he felt, made him angry. He should have put the past behind him long ago. Beginning today he would. He wouldn't think about it anymore. He wouldn't let it hurt him anymore. It was over and done.

He looked up, and there she was.

"Hello. I'm sorry I'm late," Desiree said.

His gaze shifted quickly from the scar that twisted her smile to the first place he could think to look—his watch. "You're right on time."

"I didn't think I'd make it. We were late getting up and—"

"Are you going to be my daddy?"

"Nicole!" Desiree clapped a hand over her daughter's mouth. "She's a little excited."

"So am I," Carter admitted with a wry smile. "Shall we get on with it?" He snagged Desiree by the elbow and headed in the direction of the judge's chambers. She was wearing that moth-eaten coat again. He wondered what she had on under it. He didn't have to wait long to satisfy his curiosity. The judge's chambers were uncomfortably warm, and Desiree slipped the black wool off her shoulders and laid it over the back of a brass-studded maroon leather chair.

She smiled at Carter again, and he forced his eyes down over the flowered dress she was wearing. It was obviously the best she had, but wrong for the season, and it showed years of wear. He felt a spurt of guilt for not offering her the money for a new dress. But since she apparently didn't know about his wealth, he preferred to keep it that way. Then, if feelings developed between them, he would be sure they weren't motivated by the fact he had a deep pocket.

Desiree couldn't take her eyes off Carter. She was stunned by his appearance. In the first place, he had shaved off the shadow of beard. His blunt jaw and sharp, high cheekbones gave his face an almost savage look. His tailored Western suit should have made him look civilized, but instead it emphasized the power in his broad shoulders and his over-six-foot height. "You look... wonderful," she said.

For some reason, Carter appeared distressed by the compliment. Then she realized he hadn't said anything about how she looked. It didn't take much imagination to figure out why. She had done nothing to hide the scar on her face. She had seen how his eyes skipped away from it. But he was still here. And apparently ready to go through with the wedding.

The judge entered his chambers in a flurry of black robes. "I've only got a few minutes," he said. "Are you two ready?"

"There are three of us, Judge Carmichael," Carter said, nodding in Nicole's direction.

"So there are," the judge said. He peered over the top of his black-rimmed bifocals at the little girl. "Hello there. What's your name?"

Nicole retreated behind her mother's skirts.

"Her name is Nicole," Desiree said.

"All right, Nicole. Let's get your mommy married, shall we? Why don't the two of you stand together in front of my desk?" the judge instructed Carter and Desiree. He called his secretary and the court bailiff to act as witnesses.

Desiree suddenly felt as shy as her daughter and wished there were a skirt she could retreat behind. Carter reached out to draw her to his side, but she quickly scooted around him so the unblemished part of her face would be toward him while they said their vows. She wished she could have been beautiful for him. It would have made all this so much easier. But she wouldn't have needed a husband if things had been different.

"Are we all ready?" the judge asked.

"Just a minute." Carter searched the room for a moment. "There they are." He crossed to a bookshelf and picked up a small bouquet of flowers. "When I arrived your secretary offered to put these in here for me."

Desiree stared at the bouquet of wildflowers garnished with beautiful white silk ribbons that Carter was holding out to her. A flush skated across her cheekbones. The thoughtfulness of his gesture made her feel more like a bride. It made everything seem more real. Her heart thumped a mile a minute, and she put a hand up as though to slow it down.

She stared at Carter, seeing wariness—not warmth—in his green eyes as she reached out to take the flowers. "Thank you, Carter."

His features relaxed and the wariness fled, replaced by what looked suspiciously like relief. Unfortunately, Carter's trek for the flowers had taken him across the room, and when he returned he ended up on her right side, the side with the scar. She hid her dismay, but lowered her chin so her hair fell across her face.

"Now are we ready?" the judge asked impatiently.

Desiree nodded slightly. She felt Carter's fingertips on her chin. He tipped her face upward until he was looking her in the eye.

"Are you sure you want to do this?"

"Yes," she croaked.

"Keep your chin up," he murmured. He turned to the judge and said, "We're ready."

Desiree appreciated Carter's encouraging words but had no idea how to tell him so. She heard very little of what the judge said. She was too conscious of the man standing beside her. She could smell a masculine cologne and feel the heat of him along her right side. On her other side, she was aware of Nicole's death grip on her hand.

"The ring?" the judge asked.

"Here." Carter produced a simple gold band, which he slipped on Desiree's left hand.

He turned back to the judge, who was about to continue the ceremony when Desiree said, "I have a ring for you, too."

She saw the surprise on Carter's face, but he didn't object. She fumbled in the pocket of her skirt until she found the gold band she had so painstakingly selected. She was aware of the calluses on Carter's palm and fingertips as she held his hand to slip on the ring. Desiree dared a glance at Carter's face when she saw how well it fit.

He smiled at her, and she felt her heart skip a beat. She turned to face the judge, feeling confused and flustered.

Carter took her hand in his and waited for the judge to continue. It wasn't long before he said, "I now pronounce you man and wife."

To Desiree, the wedding ceremony was over too quickly, and it didn't feel "finished." She realized the judge hadn't suggested that Carter kiss his bride. She waited, every muscle tensed, wondering if he would act on his own. A second ticked past, another, and another.

Which was when Nicole said, "Are you going to kiss Mommy now?"

"Nicole!"

Desiree's face reddened with embarrassment. She couldn't bear to look at Carter, afraid of what she would see.

The sound of a masculine chuckle was followed by the feel of Carter's hand on her unblemished cheek. She closed her eyes, flinching when she felt his moist breath against her face. She heard him make a sound of displeasure in his throat and felt his hesitation.

Desiree forced herself to stand still, waiting for the touch of his lips against hers, but her body stiffened, rejecting before it came, this sign of masculine possession.

Soft. So soft. And gentle.

Desiree's eyes flickered open, and she stared wide-eyed at the man who had just become her husband. Her breathing was erratic, and her heart was bumping madly. It hadn't been a painful kiss. Quite the contrary. Her lips had…tingled. She raised her hand toward her mouth in wonder.

Carter was staring at her, the expression on his face inscrutable. She had no idea what he was thinking.

She had married a stranger.

It was a terrifying thought, and Desiree felt the panic welling up inside her. Carter must have sensed her feelings, because he quickly thanked the judge, shook Carmichael's hand, watched as the witnesses signed the marriage certificate, in which Desiree had once again given up her maiden name of Parrish, and hustled her and Nicole out of the courthouse.

"I've made reservations for lunch at Benham's," Carter said, naming one of the fanciest restaurants in Casper.

Desiree put a hand to her queasy stomach. The last thing she wanted right now was food.

"I'm starving," Nicole piped up.

"I guess that's settled," Carter said. "Let's go eat."

"Not in a restaurant," Desiree protested. "I put a roast in the oven before I left the ranch. Please, let's go home."

"Home," Carter said. It had a wonderful sound. "All right, then. Home. I'll follow you in my pickup."

Desiree welcomed the brief respite before they sat down to their first meal as husband and wife. Once in the truck, Nicole focused her attention on Desiree's wedding bouquet, which left Desiree free to mentally compare this wedding with her first one.

She had been only eighteen years old and desperately in love with Burley Kelton. Burley had come to work as a cowhand for her father, and she had fallen hard for his broad shoulders and his rakish smile. After a whirlwind romance they had married in the First Presbyterian Church. She had worn her mother's antique-lace wedding gown and carried a pungent bouquet of gardenias.

Desiree had been a total innocent on her wedding night, naive and frightened, but so in love with Burley that she would have done anything he asked.

Only Burley hadn't asked for anything. He had taken what he wanted. Brutally. Horribly. Painfully. She didn't dare cry out for fear her parents would hear her in their room down the hall from her bedroom. So she bore her wedding night stoically. She survived, to endure even worse in the next weeks and months of her marriage.

They lived with her parents, and Burley continued working for her father. She kept up a front, refusing to let her parents know how bad things were. Then her mom and dad were killed in a freak one-car accident, and she was left alone with Burley. It was a ghastly end to what she now realized were girlish dreams of romance.

Burley told her the pain she felt when he exercised his husbandly rights was her fault. He had to work hard to find any pleasure in her, because she was frigid. He should have married a woman who had more experience, one who knew how to satisfy a man.

Even though Burley found her wanting in bed, he was insanely jealous if she so much as said hello to another man. When she suggested they might be better off apart, he became enraged and said he had taken his vows "Till death do us part!" and that he had meant them.

It had almost come to that.

Desiree stole a glance at Carter in the rearview mirror. At least she would be spared her wifely duties for a time. Maybe if she explained that he would find no joy in her, Carter might even change his mind about wanting to take her to bed.

Carter was having similar, but contrary, thoughts. In fact, he was wondering how long it would be before his wife became his wife—in the biblical sense. He had stood next to her during the short ceremony and felt her heat, smelled the soft floral fragrance that clung to her hair and clothes and felt himself forcing back the feelings of want and need that rose within him.

He had seen her flinch when he tried to kiss her after the ceremony. It wasn't the first time she had recoiled from him, either. She must have been badly treated by some man, somewhere along the line. Her father? Her husband? So what were the chances she was going to let him get anywhere near her, anytime soon? Not good, he admitted. She had said they would have to wait until they knew each other better, and she had no idea when that would be. He was willing to be patient—for a while. He couldn't help comparing this wedding with his first one.

Carter hadn't been able to keep his hands off Jeanine, and she had been equally enamored of him. They had anticipated their wedding night by about a year, and knowing what he could expect in bed had kept him aroused through most of the ceremony and reception. He had been so much in love with Jeanine that it had been difficult to force the vows past his constricted throat. Knowing the reason they were marrying had been an extra bonus as far as he was concerned.

Looking back, he realized that the tears in Jeanine's eyes hadn't been tears of joy, as she had professed. His trembling bride had been trembling for entirely different reasons than the ones he had supposed. Now he knew why she had been so miserable. If only...

Carter swore under his breath. Wishing wouldn't change the past. He was crazy to be reliving that nightmare, especially when he had just promised himself he wouldn't look back anymore. He would do better to look forward to the future with Desiree Parrish—no, now Desiree Prescott.

Carter quashed the awful thought that arose like a many-headed hydra: *This woman can't betray me. Her scarred face will keep her from tempting another man.* It wasn't the first time he had thought it, and he couldn't truly say whether the scar on her face had been a consideration when he agreed to marry her. But he was ashamed for what he was thinking and grateful that Desiree couldn't read his mind. She deserved better from the man who had just become her husband.

Carter pulled his truck up beside Desiree's pickup in back of the house. His wife and new daughter were already inside the house before he could catch up to them. If he hadn't known better, he would have said Desiree was fleeing from him. If she was, she was wasting her time. Now that they were married, there was no place for her to run.

Desiree hurried to make herself busy before Carter came inside. She turned up the furnace and slipped off her coat and Nicole's and sent her daughter upstairs to play.

Then she returned to the kitchen and waited beside the stove, her arms crossed over her chest. Carter didn't bother to knock before he opened the door and stepped inside. He didn't bother to close the door, either, just headed straight for her, his stride determined. A moment later he had swept her off her feet and into his arms.

Desiree grabbed hold of his neck, afraid for a moment he might drop her. His arms tightened around her, and she knew there was no danger of that. He headed right back outside.

"What are you doing?" she asked breathlessly, her eyes wide with trepidation.

"There's a tradition that hasn't been observed."

"What's that?"

Once he was outside, he paused long enough to glare down at her. Through clenched teeth he said, "Carrying the bride over the threshold." He turned around and marched right back into the kitchen.

Desiree was too astonished to protest. She stared up at his rigid jaw and realized again how little they knew of each other. "I'm sorry," she said. "I didn't know you felt so strongly about it, or I would have waited. But we never discussed—"

"There are a lot of things we haven't discussed. I guess it's going to take a while for us to adjust to each other."

He was still holding her in his arms. Desiree became increasingly uncomfortable, as another kind of tension began to grow between them. She recognized the signs on Carter's face. The drooping eyelids, the nostrils flared for the scent of her, the jumping pulse at his throat. She began to struggle for freedom.

"Let me go. Let me down. Now!"

His hold tightened. "What the hell's the matter with you?"

"Let me go!" she shrieked.

A moment later she was on her feet. She retreated from him several paces, until her back was against the wall. She stared at him, eyes wide, blood racing. "We agreed we would wait!" she accused.

"I only wanted a kiss," he said.

She shook her head. "No kissing, no touching, nothing until we know each other," she insisted.

Desiree watched a muscle jerk in his jaw. She knew he could force her. Burley had. She reached behind her surreptitiously with one hand, searching for a weapon on the counter. But there was nothing close by.

"What did he do to you?" Carter asked in a quiet voice.

"What makes you think—"

"Every time I move too fast you flinch like a horse that's been whipped. You're trembling like a beaten animal right now. And the look in your eyes... I've seen men facing a nest of rattlers who've looked less terrified. It doesn't take a scientist to figure out you've been mistreated. Do you want to tell me about it?"

Desiree couldn't get an answer past the lump in her throat. She lowered her eyes to avoid his searching gaze. She couldn't help jerking when he reached out a hand to her.

Carter swore under his breath. "I'm not going to hurt you," he repeated through clenched teeth.

Desiree forced herself to remain still as he reached out again for her chin and tipped it up so they were staring into each other's eyes.

"You're my wife. We'll be spending the rest of our lives together. I'm willing to wait as long as it takes for you to accept me in your bed."

"No kissing, no—"

He shook his head. "There'll be kissing, and hugging and touching. Even friends do that much."

"But—"

He cut her off by putting his lips against hers. Desiree fought the panic, reminding herself that his first kiss had been gentle. This one was no less so, just the barest touch of lips, but she felt a shock clear to her toes. It wasn't a bad feeling. Oh, no, it wasn't bad at all.

Luckily, his lips left hers just at the moment when she felt herself ready to struggle in earnest. When she opened her eyes, she saw that he hadn't retreated very far.

"Desiree?"

"Carter, I...I'm scared," she admitted in a whisper.

He drew her slowly into his arms. As his strength enfolded her she forced herself to relax. It wasn't easy. Burley had sometimes begun gently, only to lose control later.

Carter's arms remained loose around her. In a few minutes she realized she was no longer trembling, that she was almost relaxed in his embrace.

"This is nice," he murmured in her ear. "You feel good against me."

Desiree stiffened. She knew he felt her withdrawal when he said, "It's all right, Desiree. It's just a hug, nothing more. Relax, sweetheart."

He cajoled her much as he might a reluctant mare, and she found herself responding to his warm baritone voice. She laid her head against his chest and tentatively put her hands at his trim waist.

Just as she made those gestures of concession, he stepped back from her. She raised her eyes to his in confusion. She hadn't expected him to stop. But she was glad he had.

"How soon will lunch be ready?" he asked.

Desiree turned quickly to the oven. She had completely forgotten about the roast beef during the past tension-filled minutes. "It should be done shortly."

"Anything I can do to help?"

Desiree raised startled eyes to study Carter's face. "You're willing to help in the kitchen?"

"Why not?"

Burley never had. Burley had said the kitchen was woman's work. "You could set the table if you'd like."

Carter took the initiative and started hunting through cabinets for what he wanted. "Best way to find out where everything is," he explained with a cheeky grin.

"You're probably right." Desiree found herself smiling back, even though it was unsettling to see a stranger going through everything as though he had the right.

He has the right. He's your husband.

As she peeled potatoes and put vegetables in a pot on the stove, Desiree realized she had been extraordinarily lucky in her second choice of husband. Carter wasn't like Burley. He could control his passions. It was too bad he was getting such a bad bargain. She couldn't be the wife he obviously wanted and needed. She was too bruised in spirit to respond as he wished.

Desiree had planned this dinner at home because she had feared that conversation between them would be stilted, and it would be embarrassing to sit across from each other in a restaurant in total silence. However, when the three of them sat down together, things didn't turn out at all as she had expected. Carter, bless him, wasn't the least bit taciturn. He even condescended to answer several of Nicole's questions. However, when Nicole finished eating and approached Carter, Desiree realized there were limits to his tolerance.

"Can I sit on your lap?" Nicole asked.

"You're a big girl," Carter replied.

"Not too big," Nicole said, sidling up next to him. "My friend Shirley sits in her daddy's lap."

"I'm not your—"

Desiree cut him off before he could deny any relationship to her daughter. "Carter has a full stomach right now. Why don't you go upstairs to your room and play," she said.

Nicole gave Carter a look from beneath lowered lashes. "Is your stomach really full?" she demanded suspiciously.

Desiree saw the war Carter waged, the way his hands fisted. "Nicole! Go play."

Nicole's lower lip stuck out, but she knew better than to argue when her mother used that tone of voice.

The little girl had already turned to leave when Carter grabbed her under the arms and hefted her into his lap. "I suppose you can sit here for a minute," he said grudgingly.

But Desiree caught the brief, awful look of anguish in Carter's eyes as his arms closed around the little girl.

Nicole settled back against Carter's chest and chattered happily, oblivious to the undercurrents.

Over the next five minutes, Carter's face looked more and more strained, and his jaw tightened. Desiree realized there was something very wrong.

"That's enough for now, Nicole," Desiree said. "It's time for you to go upstairs and choose a book for me to read before your nap."

Carter sighed as though relieved of a great burden as he lifted Nicole from his lap and set her on her feet.

Nicole ran upstairs without a backward glance, leaving them alone at the table. Desiree waited for Carter to explain himself. To her amazement, he pretended as though nothing out of the ordinary had happened.

"If I'd know how good you can cook, I'd have jumped at that first proposal," he said.

Desiree didn't press the issue. And she chose to accept the compliment, rather than be put off by the fact Carter hadn't wanted to marry her at first. "Thank you."

"Maybe you could give me a tour of the ranch this afternoon," Carter suggested.

"Nicole usually takes a nap after lunch. I should be up there getting her settled right now. You're welcome to take a look on your own."

Carter saw the relief in Desiree's eyes at the thought they wouldn't have to spend the rest of the day together. He could see she was going to use the child as an excuse to keep them apart. It was funny, because he had planned to use ranch business with her as a way to avoid the child.

"I can wait until Nicole wakes up. We'll go then," he said.

"She'll have to come with us."

As a chaperon, Carter thought wryly. But the little girl obviously couldn't be left alone, and there was no one else around to take care of her. One or the other of them would always have to be with her. Which led him to ask, "How on earth have you managed to do the chores around the ranch and take care of Nicole at the same time?"

"Sometimes it isn't easy," Desiree admitted.

Carter thought that was probably the understatement of the century.

"All right," he said. "While Nicole's napping you can show me around the house."

She gave him a disconcerted look. Was he looking for an opportunity to get her alone in the bedroom? "There isn't much to see."

"You can show me what needs fixing. I couldn't help noticing that the faucet drips in the kitchen, and the newel post on the stairs wobbles."

Two pink spots of color appeared on her cheeks. She was thinking of bed, while he was thinking of dripping faucets! It would be funny if it weren't so humilating. "I didn't marry you to get a handy-man."

He grinned. "But isn't it lucky that I am one? Come on, Desiree, every house needs a few repairs now and then."

Her lips flattened grimly. "I'm afraid this one needs more than that."

"Oh?"

She recited a long list of problems with the house that ended, "And I'm not sure the furnace will make it through the winter."

He stared at her, stunned by the enormity of what she had been coping with on her own. No wonder she had wanted—needed—a husband. Strange as it seemed, he felt better knowing how much work the ranch needed. It was a rational explanation for why she had married him, even if she had done it in a damned havy cavy way.

He could have used his money and had repairmen do everything that needed to be done in a matter of weeks. But he didn't want her to know yet about his wealth. He wanted a chance to be needed—loved?—for himself alone. Later would be soon enough to reveal the rest.

"I guess I'll start on those repairs while Nicole is napping," he conceded finally.

"I usually do something quiet, so I won't disturb her."

"And repairing the newel post is hardly quiet." He said it as a statement, not a question.

She shook her head. He was pleased to see just the hint of a smile tease the corners of her mouth. The scar didn't pucker so badly with the smaller smile. He forced his eyes away from the mark on her face.

"All right," he said with a gusty sigh. "You can show me the ranch books this afternoon. If you don't think that would be too noisy a proposition?"

Desiree giggled. She didn't know where the sound had come from, and it certainly wasn't anything she could remember doing recently. But the look of surrender to the inevitable on Carter's face struck her as funny.

"Just let me get Nicole settled, and I'll be back to do the dishes."

"I'll do them," Carter volunteered.

"That's not necessary, I—"

"The sooner the dishes are done, the sooner we can get to those ranch books."

What Desiree heard in his voice, what she saw in his eyes was *The sooner we can be alone.*

"Maybe you'd rather take that tour of the ranch," she suggested.

Carter shook his head no. "I'd rather wait and go with you."

Desiree stood rooted where she was, pierced by a look in his blue eyes that held a wealth of promises. She wanted to warn him that she couldn't fulfill those promises. But something kept her silent. The longer it took him to figure out the truth about her sexually, the better. She dreaded the disgust she was sure would be her lot when he realized what a failure she was in bed.

Desiree took one last look over her shoulder at Carter before she left the kitchen. He was already clearing the table. Her grandmother's silver-rimmed china looked fragile in his big hands, but he moved with easy grace between the table and sink. The thought of Nicole waiting anxiously for her upstairs pulled her from the mesmerizing sight of her husband doing the dishes on their wedding day.

To Nicole's delight, Desiree read two stories. The first because she always did, the second because she was putting off the moment when she would have to rejoin Carter in the parlor, which also served as the ranch office.

When Nicole's eyelids drifted shut and her tiny rosebud mouth fell slack, Desiree realized the inevitable could be avoided no longer.

She rose and squared her shoulders like an aristocrat headed for the guillotine. It was time to begin the process of becoming a wife and partner to the stranger downstairs.

Desiree felt her legs trembling and told herself she was being foolish. There was no need to fear Carter. He was not like Burley.

Not yet. But what happens when you disappoint him in bed?

That won't be for a while yet. Carter promised—

You saw the look in his eyes when he carried you over the threshold. Was that the look of a patient man?

So he desires me. That isn't a bad thing. Especially since we're married.

Are you ready to submit to him? To trust him with the secrets of your body?

Desiree shuddered. Not yet. *Not yet.* She ignored her trembling limbs and headed downstairs to join her husband. She would just have to be firm with Carter.

Sex would have to wait.

Four

Desiree walked down the stairs, knees trembling—and found Carter sound asleep on the couch. An awkward feeling of tenderness washed over her as she stared at the sleeping man. Apparently he had needed a nap as much as Nicole. She sat down across from him in the comfortable arm chair that faced the fireplace in the parlor and searched his features.

The rugged planes of his face were less fearsome in repose. The blue shadows under his eyes suggested that he had put in some long hours the week before they were married. What had he been doing? The fact that she had no idea pointed to how much a stranger he was to her. A boyish lock of chestnut hair fell across his forehead, and she had to resist the urge to reach over and brush it back into place.

Desiree breathed a sigh of relief that her fears about confronting Carter hadn't been realized. At least, not yet. She knew she ought to get up and go do some chores, but the fire made the room seem so cozy that she settled deeper into the overstuffed chair. The house was quiet, with only the sound of the furnace doing its level best to keep up with the cold. She scooched down in the chair, put her feet up on an equally overstuffed footstool, and let her eyelids droop closed.

Desiree wasn't sure what woke her, but she had the distinct feeling she was being watched. It was a feeling she recognized, and one that caused her heart to pound so hard she could almost hear it. She took a deep breath and let it out, forcing herself to relax. Then she opened her eyes.

Carter was sitting on the couch, staring at her. At some point while she was asleep, he had changed his clothes and was now wearing jeans and a red and blue plaid shirt with his work boots.

She watched him through wary eyes without moving.

"I didn't mean to wake you," he said.

She sat up carefully. "You didn't."

"If you say so." He yawned and stretched. She was impressed again by the breadth of his chest, by the play of muscles in his shoulders and arms. He caught her looking at him and grinned. "I had hoped we'd spend some part of the day sleeping together, but I had something a little different in mind."

Desiree tensed, waiting for him to make some move to close the distance between them. But he relaxed with one arm settled along the back of the couch and hung one booted ankle across the opposite knee.

"I don't suppose we'll have time now to look at the books before Nicole is awake."

Desiree looked at her watch. "We've slept away the afternoon!"

Carter thrust all ten fingers through his hair, leaving it standing in all directions. "I guess I was more tired than I thought. It's been a tough week."

"Oh?" Desiree arched a questioning brow. "What kept you so busy?"

Carter cleared his throat. "Just some business I needed to clear up before the wedding. Nothing worth mentioning."

He was lying. Desiree didn't know why she was so sure about it, except that one moment he had been looking at her—well, not at her face, but in her direction—and the next, his gaze was focused intently on the leafy design sewn into his worn leather boots. She didn't believe in keeping secrets. It spawned distrust. But considering the fact she hadn't been totally honest with Carter, Desiree could hardly challenge him on the matter.

"What shall we do with the time until supper?" Carter asked.

Desiree was thinking in terms of chores that could be finished, when Carter suggested, "Why don't you tell me a little bit about what you've been doing in the years since we last met?"

"I wouldn't know where to start. Besides, what matters is the present and the future, not the past."

Carter pursed his lips and muttered, "If only that were true."

Desiree met Carter's gaze. His eyes held the same despairing look she had seen when he held Nicole at the dinner table. What had happened, she wondered, that had caused him so much pain? "Are you all right?"

The vulnerability in his eyes was gone as quickly as it had appeared, replaced by icy orbs that didn't invite questioning. Desiree welcomed the sight of her daughter in the doorway. "Did you have a good nap, sweetheart?"

"Uh-huh. Are we going for a ride now?" Nicole bounced over to Carter and laid her hands on his thigh, as though she had known him forever.

Desiree held her breath waiting for his reaction. It came in the form of a puff of breath Carter expelled so softly it could barely be heard. He stared at the spot where Nicole's tiny hands rested so confidently against him. He stood without touching her, and her hands of necessity fell away.

Nicole reached up to tug on the sleeve of his flannel shirt. "Can we go see Matilda first?"

"Who's Matilda?" Carter asked.

"She's my calf. She's black."

"Matilda's mother didn't survive the birth," Desiree explained quietly. "I've been keeping the calf in the barn and feeding her by hand." Desiree saw the look of incredulity on Carter's face and hurried to explain, "I—we—can't afford to lose a single head of stock."

"I had no idea things were so bad," Carter said.

"There's no danger of losing the ranch," she reassured him. "I've just been extra busy because my hired hand broke his leg and has been out of commission for nearly two months."

For reasons Desiree didn't want to explain to Carter, she hadn't been able to bring herself to hire a stranger to work for her. Which made no sense at all, considering the fact she had married one.

Nicole grabbed Carter's hand and began tugging him from the room. Desiree watched to see if he would free himself. He did, quickly shoving his hands in his back pockets. But he followed where Nicole led. She trailed the two of them from the parlor through the house to the kitchen, where they retrieved their coats, hats and gloves and headed out the kitchen door.

As usual in Wyoming, the wind was blowing. Desiree hurried to catch up to Nicole so she could pull her daughter's parka hood up over her head. Before she reached Nicole, Carter did it for her.

Desiree found his behavior with Nicole confusing, to say the least. He clearly didn't want anything to do with the little girl, but he stopped short of ignoring her. What had him so leery of children?

Desiree heard Nicole chattering and hurried to catch up. Carter had been doing fine tolerating the five-year-old, but she saw no reason to test his patience.

Thanks to the body heat of the animals inside, the barn felt almost warm in comparison with the frigid outdoors. Nicole let go of Carter's hand and raced to a stall halfway down the barn. She unlatched it and stepped inside. The tiny Black Angus calf made a bleating sound of welcome and hurried up to her.

"Matilda is hungry, Mommy," Nicole said.

"I'll fix her something right now." Desiree went to the refrigerator, where she kept the milk for the calf. She poured some out into a nursing bottle and set it in a pot of water on a hot plate nearby to warm. When she returned to the stall she found Carter down on one knee beside the calf.

"Matilda's mommy is dead," Nicole explained. "So Mommy and I have to take care of her."

"It looks like you're doing a fine job," Carter conceded gruffly.

The calf bawled piteously, and Nicole circled the calf's neck with her arms to calm it. "Mommy's getting your bottle, Matilda. Moooommy!" she yelled. "Matilda's starving!"

Desiree hustled back to the hot plate, unplugged it and retrieved the bottle. A moment later she dropped onto her knees beside the calf. Nicole took the heavy bottle from her mother and held it while the calf sucked loudly and hungrily.

Desiree met Carter's eyes over the calf's head. There was a smile on his face that had made its way to his eyes.

"This is turning out to be a great honeymoon," he said with a chuckle.

Desiree laughed. "I suppose it is a little unconventional."

"That's putting it mildly."

There was a warmth in his eyes that said he would be happy to put the train back on the rails. Desiree was amazed to find herself relaxed in his presence. However, her feelings for Carter were anything but comfortable. Her fear of men hadn't disappeared. Yet she was forced to admit that Carter evoked more than fear in her breast. She hadn't expected to be physically attracted to him. She hadn't expected to want to touch him and to want him to touch her. She hadn't expected to regret her inability to respond to him—or any man—as a woman.

Her expression sobered.

"What's wrong?" Carter asked.

She wondered how he could be so perceptive. "What makes you think anything's wrong?"

He reached out a hand and smoothed the furrows on her brow. His callused fingertips slid across her unmarked cheek and along the line of her jaw.

Desiree edged away from his touch. Her heart had slipped up to lodge in her throat, making speech impossible.

"Matilda is done, Mommy," Nicole said as she extended the empty bottle toward her mother.

Desiree lurched to her feet. "That's—" She cleared her throat and tried again. "That's good, darling." She took the bottle and Nicole's hand and hurried out of the stall. She headed for the sink in the barn and rinsed out the bottle.

Carter had started after her, but when she turned around she realized he had stopped at the stall and was examining the hinges.

"This is hanging lopsided. Do you have a pair of pliers?"

Desiree would rather have headed right back to the house, but forced herself to respond naturally. "Sure. Let me get them."

Desiree watched as Carter made a few adjustments to the stall door, tightening the bolts that held the frame in place.

"That ought to do it."

Desiree thought of the months the door had been hanging like that, when neither she nor her hired hand, Sandy, had taken the time to fix it. In a matter of minutes Carter had resolved the problem.

"Thanks," she said.

"No need to thank me. It was my pleasure."

Desiree searched his face and saw the look of satisfaction there. He was telling the truth. He had enjoyed himself. "Fortunately for you there are lots of things that need fixing around here," she said sardonically.

He headed down the aisle of the barn to return the pliers to the tool box. "I think that's enough for today, though. After all, I am still on my honeymoon."

"What's a honeymoon?" Nicole asked.

Desiree saw the smirk that came and went on Carter's face. She found the question embarrassing, especially with Carter listening to everything she was about to say. But she had made it a habit to answer any question Nicole asked as honestly as possible.

"It's the time a husband and wife spend together getting to know each other when they're first married," Desiree explained.

"Like you and Mr. Prescott," Nicole said.

Desiree brushed Nicole's bangs out of her eyes. "Yes." Desiree looked up and found Carter watching her, his eyes hooded with desire. A glance downward showed her he was hard and ready. A frisson of alarm skittered down her spine. She rose abruptly and took her daughter's hand. "I'm going to start supper," she said.

"I'll be in shortly," Carter replied in a raspy voice. "I see a few more things I can do out here, after all."

The atmosphere at supper was strained. Not that she and Carter conversed much more or less than at lunchtime, but Nicole never stopped chattering. Carter never initiated contact with Nicole, but he didn't rebuff her when she climbed into his lap after supper. If the threat of danger hadn't been hanging over her, she might actually have let herself feel optimistic about the future.

She and Carter did the dishes together, while Nicole colored with crayons at the kitchen table. It was so much a picture of a natural, normal family that Desiree wanted to cry. Her feelings of guilt for marrying Carter without telling him the whole truth forced her to excuse herself and take Nicole up to bed early the night of her wedding.

"I'll see you in the morning," she said to Carter.

She didn't know what to make of the look on his face—part desire, part regret, part something else she couldn't identify—but fled upstairs as quickly as she could.

Once in bed, she couldn't sleep. She heard Carter come upstairs, heard the shower, heard him brush his teeth, heard the toilet flush. His footsteps were soft in the hall, so she supposed he must be barefoot. She knew how cold the floor was, even with the worn runner, and wondered if his feet would end up as icy as Nicole's always did. She hoped she wouldn't be finding out too soon. As far as she was concerned, the longer it took Carter to end up in her bed, the better. Because he wasn't going to be happy with what he discovered when he got there.

Then there was silence. Desiree heard the house creak as it settled. The wind howled and whistled and rattled her windowpanes. The furnace kicked on. She closed her eyes and willed herself to sleep.

Two sleepless hours later Desiree sat bolt upright, shoved the covers off and lowered her feet over the side of the bed, searching for her slippers in the glow from the tiny night-light that burned beside her bed.

"Damn!" she muttered. "Damn!"

She had spent two hours lying there pretending to sleep. Maybe a cup of hot chocolate would help. She opened the door to her bedroom and swore again. Apparently Carter had turned off the light she always left burning in the living room. It was her own fault, because she hadn't told him to leave it on. But that meant she either had to brave the dark or turn on a light upstairs in order to see and take the risk of waking Carter.

Frankly, the darkness was less terrifying than the thought of facing a rudely awakened Carter when she was wearing a frayed silk nightgown, a chenille robe and tufted terry-cloth slippers. Desiree knew her naturally curly hair was a tumble of gnarled tresses worthy of a Medusa, and since she had washed off her makeup, her scar would be even more vivid.

She knew the spots on the stairs that would groan when stepped on. She had learned them as a child so she wouldn't awaken her parents when she snuck down to shake her Christmas presents and try to determine what they were. She slid her hand down the smooth banister, walking quietly, carefully. When she reached the bottom of the stairs, she turned on the tiny light that was usually always lit.

With the light, it was easy to make her way to the kitchen. The old refrigerator hummed as she opened it, and there was a slight clink as the bottles of ketchup and pickles on the door shifted. Even though she was careful, the copper-bottomed pot she planned to use to heat the milk clanked as she freed it from the stack in the cabinet beside the sink.

She was standing at the stove with her back to the kitchen door, when she heard footsteps in the hallway.

Someone was in the house!

Her heart galloped as she searched frantically for somewhere to hide, a place to escape. Then she realized Nicole was trapped upstairs. In order to get to her daughter she would have to confront whoever was in the house. She was halfway to the kitchen threshold, when she halted. Her hand gripped her robe and pulled it closed at the neck. She stared, wild-eyed, at the man in the doorway.

When she realized it was only Carter, bare-chested, barefoot, wearing a half-buttoned pair of frayed jeans that hung low on his hips, she almost sobbed with relief.

"Desiree? It's the middle of the night. What are you doing down here? Are you all right?"

"I couldn't sleep. I—"

He didn't wait for her explanation, just crossed the distance between them and enfolded her in his arms.

Desiree stood rigid. She was aware of the heat of him, the male scent of him. She was appalled by the way her nipples peaked when they came in contact with his naked chest. She became certain that he must be able to feel her arousal, even through the layers of cloth that covered her, when she felt the hard ridge growing in his low-slung jeans.

"Desiree," he murmured.

As his arms tightened around her, memories of the past rose up to choke her. And she panicked.

"No! Don't touch me! Let me go!" Desiree struggled to be free of Carter's constraining hold. She slapped at his face, beat at him with her fists, shoved and writhed to be free. But his hold, although gentle, was inexorable.

Desiree didn't scream. She had learned not to scream. There was no one who would come to her rescue; she would have to save herself. She continued fighting until she finally realized through her panic that although he refused to release her, Carter wasn't hurting her. At last, exhausted, she stood quivering in his arms, like a wild animal caught in a trap it realizes it cannot escape.

"There, now. That's better," Carter crooned. "Easy now. Everything's gonna be all right now. You're fine. You're just fine."

As Desiree recovered from her dazed state, she became aware that Carter was speaking in a low, husky voice. She was being held loosely in his arms, and his hands were rubbing her back as though she were a small child. She looked up and saw the beginning of a bruise on his chin and the bloody scratches on his face and froze.

"I hurt you," she said.

"You've got a wicked right," he agreed with a smile. He winced as the smile teased a small cut in his lip.

"I'm so sorry."

He looked at her warily. "Would you like to explain what that commotion was all about?"

"No."

His blue eyes narrowed. "No?"

"No." For a moment she thought he wasn't going to let her evade his question.

Then he sniffed and said, "Something's burning."

"My hot chocolate!" When she pulled away, he let her go. Desiree hurried to the stove, where the milk had burned black in the bottom of the pan. "Oh, no. Look at this mess!" She retrieved a pot holder and lifted the pot off the stove and settled it in the sink.

"You can make some more."

"I don't think I could sleep now if I drank a dozen cups of hot chocolate," Desiree said in disgust.

"I heard a noise, and I came down to check it out," Carter said in a crisp voice. "You're the one who went crazy."

"I didn't—" Desiree cut herself off. Although she didn't like the description, it fit her irrational behavior. She shoved a hand through her long brown hair and crossed the room to slump into one of the kitchen chairs. "Good Lord! I can't imagine what you must think of me."

Carter joined her at the table, turning a chair around and straddling it so he was facing her. "Do you think it would help to talk about it?"

Desiree wondered how much she should tell him. And how little he would settle for knowing. "My first marriage was a disappointment," she admitted.

"I guessed something of the sort. How long were you married?"

"Two years. Then we divorced."

"I was married for five years."

"You were married?" Desiree didn't know why she was so surprised. But she was. Suddenly she had a thought. Perhaps there was a good reason, after all, for Carter's strange, distant behavior toward Nicole.

"Do you have children?"

"I have...had a five-year-old daughter. She died along with my wife in a car accident six years ago."

"I'm so sorry." No wonder he didn't want to be around Nicole! Her daughter must be an awful reminder of his loss. Desiree knew there really was no comfort she could offer, except to share with him her own grievous loss. "My parents died the same way."

"I'm sorry," he said.

A tense silence fell between them. Both wanted to ask more questions. But to ask questions was to suggest a willingness to answer them in return. And neither was ready to share with the other the secrets of their past.

It was Carter who finally broke the silence between them, his voice quiet, his tone as gentle as Desiree had ever heard it.

"If I'm going to get anything accomplished tomorrow I ought to get some sleep. But I don't feel comfortable leaving you down here alone. Is there any chance you could sleep now?"

Quite honestly, Desiree thought she would spend the rest of the night staring at the ceiling. But she could see that Carter wasn't going to go back to bed until she was settled. "I guess I am a little tired."

"I'll follow you upstairs," he said.

Desiree rose and headed for the kitchen door. Before she had taken two steps, Carter blocked her way.

"I don't know what to do to make you believe that I'd never hurt you," he said.

"I... I believe you."

Nevertheless, she flinched as he raised a hand to brush the hair away from her face.

His lips flattened. "Yeah. Sure."

Desiree cringed at the sarcasm in his voice and fled up the stairs as fast as she could. Behind her she heard the steady barefoot tread of her husband. She hurried into her bedroom and shut the door behind her. She leaned back against the door and covered her face with her hands.

I hate you, Burley. I hate what you did to me. I hate the way you made me feel. And I hate the fact that I can never be a woman to the man I married today.

Hating didn't help. Desiree had learned that lesson over the six long years since she had divorced Burley and gone on with her life. But she hadn't been able to let go of the hate—or the fear.

Because she knew that when he got out of prison in two weeks, Burley would be coming back.

Five

Christmas was a bittersweet event. They went to the candlelight service on Christmas Eve as a family and received the warm wishes and congratulations of the congregation on their marriage. Some of the women with whom Desiree had worked on the Christmas pageant over the past couple of years knew that Burley was due to be released from prison soon. Desiree saw the knowledge in their eyes of why she had so hurriedly married a man she barely knew. She was grateful that none of them mentioned the fact to Carter.

Nicole fell asleep on the ride home, and Desiree carried her right upstairs to bed. Carter didn't offer to help her, and Desiree didn't bother to ask. She had seen how uncomfortable he was in church, and from the moment they left the service he had been uncommonly silent. She knew he must be remembering his family—his first wife and his daughter.

While she dressed Nicole for bed and slipped her daughter under the covers, Desiree debated whether to join Carter downstairs. She pictured his face as it had looked when lit solely by candlelight during the church service. He must have loved his wife very much to still be so sad six years after her death. Of course, Desiree could identify with his despair at the loss of his daughter. After all, hadn't she been willing to make any sacrifice to ensure Nicole's safety?

By the time she had finished her musings she was already at the bottom of the stairs. She took the few steps farther to the parlor, where the wonderful-smelling spruce Christmas tree forced an acknowledgment of the season, expecting to see Carter there. But the room was empty.

Desiree went in search of her husband. It amazed her to realize that she had been so wrapped up in her own agony over the past six years that she hadn't focused on the fact that there must be others in similar straits. In fact, she had seen with her own eyes that Carter Prescott was fighting demons of the past equally as ferocious as her own. Her heart went out to him. Comfort was something she could offer in repayment for the security she hoped this marriage would provide for her and her daughter.

She found Carter in the kitchen. Desiree couldn't help the bubble of laughter that escaped when she realized he was fixing the dripping faucet.

"What's so funny?" Carter demanded.

"You. It's Christmas Eve. What on earth are you doing?"

"Fixing the faucet."

"I can see that," Desiree said as she approached him. "What I want to know is why now?"

Carter shrugged. "You were busy. There was nothing else to do."

"You could have sat down in the living room and relaxed."

"I don't like sitting still. It leaves me with too much time to think."

"About your wife and daughter?" When Desiree saw the way his shoulders stiffened she wished she had kept her thoughts to herself.

"They were killed on Christmas Eve," Carter said in a quiet voice. "They were on the way to church. I...I wasn't with them. I was at my office when I heard what had happened." He gave a shuddering sigh. "I don't think I'll ever forget that night."

Desiree followed the impulse to comfort that had brought her seeking Carter in the first place. She put a hand on his arm and felt the muscles tighten beneath her fingertips. "I don't know what to say."

He threw the wrench he was using on the counter and turned to face her. "I'd rather not talk about it," he said brusquely.

"You aren't the first man to put business before family," she replied. "It wasn't your fault the accident happened."

"I said I don't want to talk about it."

His voice was harsh and his face savage. Instead of fleeing him, Desiree stepped forward and circled his waist with her arms. She laid her head against his chest, where she could hear the furious pounding of his heart. "I'm glad you came to Wyoming," she said. "I'm glad you agreed to marry me. I'm glad you're here."

She could feel his hesitation and knew he was trying to decide whether to thrust her away or accept the comfort she was offering. She had her answer when his arms circled her shoulders, and he pulled her snug against him.

Desiree forced herself to relax. There was nothing loverlike in his demeanor or in hers. She was simply one human being offering comfort on Christmas Eve to another.

Only it wasn't that simple.

She should have known it wouldn't be. He was a man. She was a woman. As much as she tried to ignore the fact, as much as she was appalled by it, her body responded to the closeness of his.

Desiree had believed, after her experience with Burley, that there was something wrong with her, that she was defective somehow, that she didn't have whatever was necessary to make her physically responsive to a man. But ever since she had met Carter, she had been discovering that her body was more than responsive. Her blood pumped, her body ached deep inside, her breasts felt heavy and her nipples peaked whenever she was close to him. All the signs of arousal were there.

She was simply too terrified of what might—or might not—happen to allow anything to go forward. What if she was wrong? What if she couldn't respond?

"Thank you, Desiree," Carter murmured. "I didn't know how much I needed a hug."

The feel of his warm breath in her ear made her shiver. "I guess I know a little of what you're feeling," she murmured back.

He chuckled. "If you knew what I'm feeling right now you'd run up those stairs and lock your bedroom door behind you."

Desiree took a tremulous breath. "Carter?"

"What?"

"You can kiss me, if you want."

She heard him catch his breath, felt the tenseness in the muscles of his back where her hands rested. He lifted his head to look at her, but she lowered her gaze so he couldn't see that there was as much fear as anticipation lurking in her brown eyes.

"What brought this on?"

"I don't know," she mumbled. "I just thought—"

"I guess I shouldn't look a gift horse in the mouth."

Before Desiree had a chance to change her mind, his fingertip caught her chin and tipped her mouth up so it could meet his.

As with each of their two previous kisses, his mouth was gentle on hers. He cherished her with his touch. There was none of the pain she had come to expect from Burley.

"Desiree?"

She looked up at him through lids that were heavy with desire. "Yes, Carter?"

He smiled. "I keep waiting for the scratching tiger to show her claws. Are you sure you want to do this?"

"Could we just kiss, Carter? Without the touching, without anything else? I think I would like that."

She could see the rigid control in his body as he considered the scrap she had offered him in place of a Christmas feast. She wanted to offer more, but it was taking every ounce of courage she had to stand still within his embrace.

"All right, Desiree. Just kisses."

She expected him to focus on her mouth, but his lips dropped to her throat, instead.

"Ohhh." She shivered at the warmth and wetness of his lips and tongue against the tender flesh beneath her ear. He sucked just a little, and she felt her insides draw up tight. "Ohhh."

He chuckled as his mouth wandered up the slender column of her throat toward her ears. "You sound so surprised. What were you expecting?"

"Nothing like this," Desiree assured him with a gasp. "It feels...I never..."

She felt him pause. She was afraid her confession might make him stop, so she quickly said, "I like what you're doing. Very much."

His teeth caught the lobe of her ear and nibbled gently.

Desiree thought her knees were going to buckle right then and there. She laughed in delight and grabbed handfuls of Carter's shirt. One of his arms slipped around her waist and tightened, while the other remained around her shoulders. Instead of feeling imprisoned, she merely felt supported.

Now his tongue was tracing the shell of her ear, then dipping inside, before his teeth found her earlobe again. She shivered once more and realized it was becoming harder to catch her breath.

"Shouldn't I be kissing you, too?" she asked.

"In a minute," Carter rasped.

Desiree wanted to reciprocate in some way, and if he wasn't going to let her kiss him back, that left her with the option of caressing him with her hands. She felt at a distinct disadvantage. Burley hadn't been much interested in foreplay, so she didn't have any experience in arousing her partner. She wasn't sure what would please Carter. If she'd had more nerve, she would have asked him. But that was more than she could handle. She decided to experiment.

Desiree began by letting her hands slide up his back, feeling the play of muscle and sinew as she went. The sound of pleasure he made deep in his throat was all she needed to assure her that he enjoyed her touch. To her relief, although his grip on her tightened, his hands remained where they were.

His lips kissed their way across her unblemished cheek toward her mouth. He kissed one edge, then the other, then pressed his mouth lightly against hers. His tongue slid along the crease, which tickled and tingled at the same time.

"Desiree, open your mouth for me."

She felt his lips moving against hers as he spoke. She opened her mouth to answer him, but he must have thought she was responding to his request, because the instant her lips parted, his tongue slipped inside.

Desiree jerked her head away. She was panting, as though she had run a long race. And ashamed, because she had let her past fears rule once again. When Burley had kissed her like that, his tongue had thrust so hard and deep into her mouth that it had nearly gagged her.

Because she still had her hands on Carter's waist, she could feel the rigid displeasure in his body at her retreat. "I . . . I don't like to be kissed like that," she explained.

"What is it you don't like?"

Desiree's eyes flashed to his. She hadn't expected to be asked for details. It was too humiliating to tell the truth. "I . . . I just don't like it."

"All right," Carter said. "I can accept that you don't like being kissed openmouthed."

Desiree sagged with relief in his arms.

That is, until he continued, "But I do like it. So, if I can't kiss you like that, you'll have to kiss me."

"Like that?" Desiree asked. "You mean putting my tongue in your mouth?"

He laugh ruefully. "Not all at once. A little bit at a time."

Desiree cocked her head skeptically. "Are you sure you'll like it?"

His husky laugh was infectious. "I'm sure."

"What if I do it wrong?"

"There isn't any right or wrong. Just what feels good to you."

"If I just concentrate on my own feelings, how will I know you're enjoying yourself?" she asked with asperity.

"Don't worry," he assured her. "I'm sure I'll manage fine."

Desiree knew there was a catch somewhere in his reasoning, but she was so intrigued by the idea of being the one in control of the kiss that she was willing to go along with his plan. Her hand crept up to circle his neck and angle his head down for her kiss. He bent to her, and she pressed her lips against his. To her surprise, he kept his lips sealed.

She settled back on her heels and looked at him in consternation. "I thought you wanted me to kiss you."

"I do."

"Then why didn't you open your mouth?"

"You didn't open yours."

"How do you know that?"

"Well, did you?"

She grimaced. "All right. Let's try this again." Desiree put her hands flat against Carter's chest and rose on her toes to reach his mouth, careful to keep her lips parted. When they touched, she let her tongue slip into his mouth. A shiver shot down her spine. She retreated and looked up at him through lowered lashes. His lips were damp where they had kissed.

"Again?" she asked.

He nodded.

This time, she leaned her body into his so her breasts brushed against his chest. She threaded both hands into his hair and used her hold to tug his head down so she could reach his mouth. His lips were sealed again. She ran her tongue along the seam of his lips, as he had done with her. His lips parted. Tentatively she slipped her tongue into his mouth.

He groaned, a purely male sound of satisfaction.

She waited for him to take control of the kiss from her, to thrust his tongue in her mouth. But he held himself still. He left the seduction to her.

Heady with a sense of feminine power, she used her tongue to taste him, to feel his teeth and the roof of his mouth and his rough tongue. She heard his ragged breathing and knew he was aroused by what she was doing to him. What amazed her was the fact that she was equally aroused by the intimate kisses.

She withdrew her tongue and nibbled on his lower lip. His hands clutched her more tightly, but he didn't make a move toward her breasts or bottom. He exercised a rigid control on himself that gave her the confidence to continue her experiment.

"Desiree."

"What, Carter?"

"You're killing me."

"You want me to stop?"

"Hell, no! But let me kiss you back. Please."

Desiree thought about it a moment. "No. Not yet."

She watched his Adam's apple bob as he swallowed hard.

"All right," he said. "I'm putty in your hands."

Desiree grinned. The rock hard muscles in his shoulders were anything but malleable. But his mouth, as she touched it with her own, was as soft as she could wish.

As she practiced kissing him, using her tongue to tease and taste him, she was able to think less about what she was doing and more about what she was feeling. Soon her breathing was as ragged as his, her body hot and achy with need. She had kept herself separated from Carter from the waist down, not wishing to incite him to anything more than the kisses she had promised. But the instinctive need to arch her body into his became too hard to resist.

She knew the instant her belly brushed against the ridge in his jeans that she had made a mistake. The harsh, ragged sound he made was as wild as anything she had ever heard. She knew she should withdraw, but the teasing heat of him drew her back, and she rubbed herself against him, liking the feeling that streaked from her belly to her breasts to her brain.

It took her a moment to realize that his tongue was in her mouth. And that she craved having it there. He withdrew and penetrated again, mimicking the sexual act with his mouth and tongue.

Desiree had never felt anything so erotic in her entire life. She heard a guttural sound and realized it had come from her own throat. It was a sound of primitive animal need. It scared the hell out of her.

She tore herself from Carter's arms and stumbled back a step or two. She stared at him wide-eyed, panting to catch her breath, her body shuddering with unfulfilled need, her breasts swollen and aching to be touched.

"Desiree?"

Just that one word, said in a voice that demanded her attention like pebbles thrown at a windowpane. It was a plea. It was a prayer. It was an invitation she found hard to resist.

She knew, deep in her soul, that with Carter things were going to be different. After all, she had never felt anything with Burley like she had just experienced with Carter. But what if, when he bedded her, she stiffened and froze? What if she was dry inside as she had been with Burley? What if sex with Carter hurt her and disappointed him?

The risks were too great, and the rewards too uncertain. She had offered a kiss, and he had accepted. It wasn't her fault things had gotten out of hand. Well, not *all* her fault.

"I think that's enough for now." She waited with her weight balanced on the balls of her feet, her hands clenched into fists, ready to flee—or fight—if he sought more from her.

"All right, Desiree. I guess I'll be heading off to bed. It's bound to be an early morning if Nicole is anything like..."

"Like your daughter?"

He swallowed hard and nodded.

"Good night, Carter."

He didn't say anything more, just whirled on his bootheels and left the kitchen. She heard his heavy tread on the stairs and his muffled steps as he headed down the carpeted hall to his bedroom.

Desiree heaved a sigh of relief, followed by a groan of dissatisfaction. If only she had been able to follow through on what she had started, she might be lying in Carter's arms right now. She was certain the experience would be nothing like it had been with Burley. The little bit of kissing she had done with Carter had been a mistake, because now she would want more. And so would he.

She didn't want to admit it, but anything that tied her more closely to Carter was important because of the confrontation she knew was coming. That might mean swallowing her fear and submitting to Carter's desire—although even that thought did not seem so horrid as it once had.

It took Desiree a long time to fall asleep that night. Her dreams were all of a chestnut-haired man with broad shoulders and narrow hips who held her close and made tempestuous, passionate—but always gentle—love to her.

Desiree was still half-aroused when she awoke to the sound of her daughter's laughter drifting up the stairs. It was followed by a masculine rumble. She hurried to throw on her robe and stuff her feet into her slippers. She practically ran down the stairs and moments later entered the parlor, where she found Carter and Nicole sitting cross-legged beside the Christmas tree.

A fire crackled in the fireplace, and snowflakes drifted lazily down outside the picture window. The decorative lights on the tree sparkled, and there were dozens of presents under the tree—many more than had been there when she had gone to bed last night.

"Mommy! Santa Claus came!" Nicole scrambled up and headed toward her on the run.

Desiree caught her daughter and swung her up into her arms. She carried Nicole back to where Carter still sat beside the tree. "Where did all these presents come from?"

"Santa Claus!" Nicole said. "He came! He came!"

Desiree tried to get Carter to meet her gaze, but he was already reaching for a present. Nicole struggled to be put down, and Desiree slid her down until her feet hit the floor. Nicole reached Carter in three hops and bounced down into his lap.

Desiree saw him stiffen only slightly before he accepted Nicole's closeness.

"Can we open presents now, Mommy?"

"I guess so."

Desiree started to sit on the couch, but Carter patted the braided rug beside him and said, "You don't want to be way over there. Come sit beside us."

"Yeah, Mommy. Come sit beside us."

Desiree raised a brow at the "us" but couldn't resist the invitation. "Sure." She settled cross-legged beside them and waited with as much excitement as Nicole while her daughter picked up one of the presents that had miraculously appeared under the tree overnight and shook it.

"Legos, Mommy! Legos!"

"How do you know?" Desiree asked with a grin.

By then Nicole had torn the paper off, revealing the Legos she had identified by sound.

While Nicole oohed and aahed over her present, Carter handed Desiree a box with a big red bow. "Here's one for you."

"Look at all these presents! Carter, you shouldn't have!"

"What shouldn't Carter have done, Mommy?" Nicole asked.

Desiree had maintained the illusion of Santa Claus for her daughter because she believed it was a harmless fiction. So she hesitated before chastising Carter for buying so many gifts that as far as her daughter knew had all come from Santa Claus. Carter must have spent a fortune! Desiree was certain it was money he didn't have, which made his gesture all the more touching.

"Uh... Carter shouldn't have given me a present to open before you finished opening yours," Desiree said, improvising.

"I'm done now, Mommy. Open yours!"

From the look on his face, Carter was enjoying himself. After the things he had told her about his daughter, Desiree was glad he was able to bring himself to share this Christmas morning with them. It would be churlish for her to diminish what he had done by making an issue of the money he must have spent. She gave Carter a timid smile and began ripping the paper off her gift.

Her mouth split wide in a grin of delight. "How did you know I wanted this?" She held up the bulky knit sweater against herself and ran her hands over the sections of the bodice where different textures—leather and fur and feathers—had been woven into the sandy beige garment to give it an earthy look.

"I have to confess I asked my grandmother."

"How did Maddy know? I'm sure I never said anything to her about this sweater."

"I believe she heard about it from one of the ladies at church."

"Thank you," Desiree said with a shy smile.

Nicole had already helped herself to another present. "Look, Mommy!" It was a furry stuffed animal, a black cat with white paws that looked remarkably like Boots. "My very own kitten."

Nicole hugged the cat. "You open one, Daddy."

The color bleached from Carter's face. His smile disappeared, and a muscle jerked in his cheek as he clenched his teeth.

"Daddy?"

Desiree quickly scooped Nicole out of Carter's lap and into hers. She wasn't sure what to say. Apparently Nicole's innocent slip had reminded him of his child. She recognized his distress but was helpless to ease it.

"Carter?"

An instant later he was on his feet. "I need a cup of coffee. You two go on without me." He was gone from the room before Desiree had a chance to ask him to stay.

"What's the matter with Daddy?" Nicole asked.

Trust the child to know that all wasn't as it should be. Desiree was left with the unpleasant task of providing an answer that would appease her daughter. "I guess he just needs a cup of coffee."

"But we're opening presents!" Nicole protested. "He should be here." She rose with the evident intent of following Carter into the kitchen. Before she got very far they heard the back door open and close. Nicole ran into the kitchen. Desiree followed her.

"Where is Daddy going?" Nicole asked.

"I don't know, darling."

"When is he coming back?"

"I don't know."

"I want to open my presents," Nicole said. "Do we have to wait for Daddy to come back?"

Desiree felt a surge of anger that Carter should have left so abruptly without a word of explanation, and on Christmas morning! Running away wouldn't ease his pain, only postpone it. She and Nicole would still be here when he came back. If he came back. Desiree shoved a hand through her hair in frustration. She had been as much caught off guard as Carter was by Nicole's ready acceptance of him as her father. They should have realized what Nicole's reaction was likely to be. Nicole knew nothing about Burley, so there was no male figure to whom she had previously given her affection.

And after all, Nicole *had* asked for a daddy for Christmas, and Carter *had* conveniently appeared.

Nicole tugged at her sleeve. "Mommy?"

"I don't think Carter will mind if we go ahead without him. We can show him all our gifts when he comes back. How does that sound?"

"Okay!" Nicole said. She raced back to the parlor.

Desiree stared out the kitchen window and saw the tread marks left in the snow by Carter's pickup. "He will come back," she murmured to herself.

Meanwhile, Carter had driven hell-for-leather several miles from the ranch before he calmed down enough to realize how badly he had acted. He pulled to the side of the road and stopped the truck. His head fell forward to the steering wheel, and he groaned.

"What have I done? What am I doing here?"

He had only been fooling himself to think he would be able to ignore having a five-year-old child in the house. From the very first day, Nicole had made it plain she expected him to be a father to her.

What amazed and appalled him was how quickly she had slipped past the walls he had set up to keep himself from caring—to keep himself from being hurt again. When Nicole had called him "Daddy," it had set off all those painful memories of Christmases with his daughter, along with a feeling of bitter regret that his child was dead. Far worse, it had brought a lump of feeling to his throat to find himself adopted by the fatherless little girl in his arms.

He had glanced at Desiree and seen the pity—and sympathy—in her eyes. And felt ashamed that he wasn't able to handle the situation better. After all, she was willing to try marriage—and intimacy— again even though it was clear she had suffered at her husband's hands. She was dealing with her demons. Could he do less?

His feelings were complicated by the fact he had always wanted children, and Nicole was an adorable child. Nevertheless, it wouldn't be easy to play the role of father. He grimaced. It was no more difficult for him to be a father, than for Desiree to play the role of wife.

Carter didn't choose to examine his feelings for Desiree too closely. For now it was enough that he desired her, that he admired her courage and that she was the mother of the child who wanted him to be her father. Putting down roots meant having a family. He had the start of that family with Desiree and Nicole. He would be a fool not to embrace them both.

He twisted the key and turned the truck around.

They were still opening presents twenty minutes later when Carter reappeared. He stood in the parlor doorway with what could only be described as a sheepish look on his face.

"Did I miss anything?"

Desiree was too astonished that he had returned so quickly to speak. Nicole more than made up for her silence.

"Daddy! Daddy! Look what I got!"

Desiree thought for a moment he was going to run again. Though his face blanched and his jaw tightened, he stood his ground as Nicole came barreling toward him. He scooped her up and balanced her in the crook of his arm as she babbled on about the

Raggedy Ann doll and the Teenage Mutant Ninja Turtle puzzle and the game of Chutes and Ladders she had gotten from Santa Claus.

"You'll never guess what Santa Claus brought Mommy!" she exclaimed.

"What?" Carter asked.

"A teeny tiny nightgown! And you can see right through it!"

Carter grinned. "You don't say!"

Desiree felt herself flush to the roots of her hair. She hadn't realized how revealing the negligee was until she held it up to look at it. She had quickly stuffed it back into the box, but not before Nicole had gotten a look at it.

"Are you going to open your presents now, Daddy?"

Desiree saw the mixed feelings that flashed across his face.

"There are presents for me?"

"Uh-huh." Nicole held up three fingers, then put one down. "Two of them."

"Guess I'd better open them and see what I got."

He carried Nicole back over to the tree. He held on to her when he sat down cross-legged, so she was once more sitting in his lap. Desiree couldn't help but wonder what had caused Carter's acceptance of a situation she knew was painful for him.

She watched with bated breath as Carter opened the present she had bought for him. She breathed a sigh of relief when she saw the pleasure on his face as he caught sight of the Western leather boots.

"These are beautiful," he said as he reverently ran his fingers across the tooled brown leather. "You shouldn't have. I can imagine these set you back a pretty penny."

"I wanted to get them for you," Desiree said to keep him from focusing on the cost of the boots. They were expensive, but she had seen how the heels and toes, not to mention the soles, were worn on his boots. If he could have afforded to replace them, she knew he would have. She didn't want him focusing on the difference in their financial situations. She knew he hadn't married her for her money. Her land, yes. But not her money.

"Open the other one," Nicole urged as she handed it to him. "This one's from me," she confided. "For my new daddy."

Desiree saw Carter's hesitation. He slowly unwrapped the gift.

Before he had the paper half off Nicole blurted, "It's a book. So you can read stories to me at bedtime."

Carter finished upwrapping the present and fingered the embossed illustration on the cover. "It's a wonderful gift, Nicky."

"My name isn't Nicky. It's Nicole."

"Would you mind if I shortened it, sort of like a special nickname?" Carter asked.

Nicole wrinkled her nose, then eyed Carter sideways. "Will that make me your little girl for real and always?"

A sudden thickness appeared in Desiree's throat. Tears blurred her eyes and made her nose burn. She waited to hear what Carter would answer.

"It makes you mine, Nicky. Now and always."

"All right," Nicole said. "You can call me Nicky." She turned to her mother. "Daddy's going to call me Nicky. You can call me Nicky, too."

"All right, Nico—Nicky. If that's what you want." Desiree fought back the sudden spurt of jealousy she felt. She had wanted Nicole to have a father, but she hadn't realized at the time what that would mean. She no longer had her daughter all to herself.

Nicole was looking at Carter with what could only be described as worship. It remained to be seen how long her daughter's adoration would last.

Desiree stood and reached over to grasp Nicole's hands and pull her to her feet. "Now that all the presents are opened, I'd like some time to talk to Carter alone. Why don't you take a few of your things upstairs and play for a while?"

"All right, Mommy. Will you come read to me later, Daddy?"

"Sure, Nicky."

When the little girl was gone, Desiree paced away from Carter to stare out the window at the snow, which was now blowing sideways. "Where did you go?"

She was startled when his voice came from right behind her.

"Five miles down the road. It took me that long to realize it was foolish to run away from what I've been searching for all my life."

Desiree whirled to face him. She probed his blue eyes, looking for some kind of proof that she and Nicole were that important to him. "I know it must have been hard to have Nicole call you Daddy."

He nodded.

"Thank you for giving her the chance to have a father."

"I want us to be a family," Carter said in a fierce voice. "I want us to be happy together. I want to forget the past."

But it was clear from the agitation in his voice that though he might choose not to remember the past, he hadn't forgotten it. Not by a long shot.

Desiree knew she ought to take advantage of this moment to tell him the secret she had been keeping from him. But she didn't want to spoil the moment.

He was offering to start over with her. She so much wanted this marriage to work!

"I want what you want, Carter," she admitted.

But her arms remained folded defensively across her chest.

He reached for her wrists and pulled her arms around his waist. He circled her shoulders so she found herself captured in his strong embrace. She waited for the fear to rise. It was marvelously absent. But she wasn't entirely comfortable, either. There was a tension, an expectation, an awareness that arced between them. She waited for Carter to act on it, to make a sexual overture.

Instead he stepped back from her and took her hands in his. She looked up at him and found his lips curled into a smile, his blue eyes twinkling with amusement.

"So you can see right through that nightgown. I can hardly wait!"

Desiree yanked her hands from his and perched them on her hips. "How could you give me a gift like that and not warn me about it? I was never so embarrassed in my life as when Nicole started asking me questions about it."

"What did you tell her, I wonder?" Carter said as his smile broadened to a grin.

Desiree felt the heat in her face. "That it was meant to be worn with a robe," she snapped.

Carter laughed, a sound that came up from his belly and rumbled past his chest. "When am I going to get to see it?"

"In your dreams, Prescott," she said. "In your dreams!"

"I'm sure they'll be sweet ones," he called to her retreating back.

Six

"Do you want to go?" Carter asked.

"I'm not sure we can," Desiree replied across the breakfast table. "I don't know whether I can get a baby-sitter on such short notice. Especially when tonight is New Year's Eve."

Desiree knew she was being contrary, but she couldn't help it. Ever since Carter had walked out on Christmas morning, she had worried that he would do it again. Even though he had returned, the trust she had been willing to give him without question when they married was qualified now. Her anxiety wasn't unjustified.

Carter hadn't disappeared without a word over the past week, but he had begun making forays around the ranch by himself, getting the lay of the land and looking the place over. He hadn't reissued the invitation he had made the day they were married to survey the ranch together.

Desiree suspected he needed the time alone to come to terms with his new responsibilities as husband and father—although they were more *father* than *husband* so far. To her chagrin, Desiree realized she very much wanted to make the effort to become Carter's wife in every sense of the word. Only she wasn't sure how to let him know.

Attending a New Year's Eve party at Faron and Belinda Whitelaw's home would be their first outing as husband and wife. The truth was, she wanted to go. But she was worried about leaving Nicole home alone with a baby-sitter. Burley was due to be released from prison today. There was no reason to believe he would head straight for Casper—except the threats he had made six years ago.

I'm coming back, Desiree. Then I'll finish what I started.

Desiree felt cold all over. She hadn't forgotten the last night she had spent with Burley in this house. It was something she had been trying to forget. Maybe it wasn't such a bad idea to be gone from here tonight. But she wanted Nicole where she could keep an eye on her.

"I suppose we could take Nicole with us," Desiree mused. "She could sleep upstairs at The Castle. I've done that in the past when I couldn't find a sitter."

"Great!" Carter said.

"Why are you so anxious to go to this party?" Desiree asked.

"I thought it was about time we did some socializing with our neighbors. Besides, it's a wedding celebration for my half brother, Faron. He and Belinda were married at home on Christmas, with just their families present."

"You're family. Why weren't you invited to the wedding?"

He shrugged. "I was, but I decided not to go."

"Were you worried that they might be upset at how quickly you married me?"

"Not at all. It's just that Faron and I may be related, but really, we don't know each other."

Desiree's lips curled into a wry smile. "The same thing could be said about us."

"Yeah, but I'm planning to spend the rest of my life with you."

Desiree hoped so. But she had her doubts about what Carter would do when he knew the truth about why she had married him.

When she had ruthlessly sought out a man to marry, she had done so because when Burley got out of prison and came hunting her she wanted her ex-husband to see that she had committed herself to someone else, that there was no sense in his pursuing her any longer. Now she admitted to herself that she had expected to get something else out of the bargain: actual physical protection if Burley got violent.

Desiree could see how her fear and desperation had led her to expect unrealistic things from marriage to Carter. Instead of being put off by the presence of another man, Burley was just as likely to become insanely jealous. It had happened before. And she knew that instead of being around to protect her, Carter might very well be off on one of his lonely jaunts around the ranch.

Which meant she had to be ready to protect herself and her daughter. She couldn't get a protective order to keep Burley away from her until he had actually done something that constituted a crime under the law. She would have to wait for Burley to make the first move. And hope she was still alive to apply to the court for succor.

There was another option.

She could confess the whole situation to Carter and ask for his help in confronting Burley when he showed up. She felt certain Carter would offer his assistance if he knew the situation she was in. But she had her own reasons for wanting to keep her secret as long as she could.

Ever since Christmas Eve, when she had stood in Carter's arms kissing him, the belief had been growing that maybe she wasn't as frigid as Burley had always accused her of being. She had thought and thought about her reaction to Carter's kisses, about her feelings when kissing him, and she had come to the conclusion that however much a failure she had been with Burley in bed, the same thing wouldn't happen with Carter.

Desiree wasn't sure what made the difference with Carter. She didn't think it was a simple matter of her feelings toward the two men. After all, she had been head over heels in love with Burley and sex with him had been a disaster. She wasn't sure exactly what she felt for Carter, but she knew it couldn't be love. Respect, maybe, and liking, but no more than that. After all, they were still virtual strangers.

Once the idea of making love to Carter caught hold, however, she couldn't let it go. She fantasized about what it would be like to touch him, to have him touch her, for the two of them to be joined as one. Since she couldn't be sure what Carter's reaction would be when he found out the truth about why she had married him, she had to act soon or perhaps lose the chance of knowing what it meant to make love to a man.

Maybe it wasn't fair to use Carter like that, but Desiree had gotten the distinct impression that he wouldn't find making love to her a hardship. They would both benefit, and she couldn't see the harm to either of them in her plan.

Only... time was running out. If she was going to seduce Carter, there could be no better opportunity than after the party tonight. It would be the beginning of a new year, a nostalgic time, to say the least. She would make sure Carter had a drink or two to relax him and would stay very close when they danced. And she would wear the silky black negligee he had given her for Christmas. Further than that, her thoughts would not go.

"So we're agreed?" Carter said. "We'll go to the party?"

Desiree nodded. "I'll call Belinda so she can arrange a guest bedroom for Nicole."

Desiree wasn't sure what to expect from her friends and neighbors at the Whitelaws' New Year's Eve party, but she was pleased by how cordially they greeted Carter when she introduced him as her husband.

Carter's grandmother, Madelyn, made a special point of introducing one young woman to Carter. "This is Belinda's sister, Fiona Conner," she said. "I'm disappointed you two didn't get a chance to meet sooner."

Unspoken were the words *Before you married Desiree.*

Desiree felt an unwelcome stab of jealousy as the petite blond gave Carter an assessing look. She immediately forgave Fiona when the young woman grinned at her and said, "Maddy tells me she had Carter all picked out for me, so I'm glad you two found each other. You've saved me from Maddy's matchmaking."

"It was my pleasure," Desiree said, linking her arm possessively through Carter's. She was aware of how lovely the young woman was. There was no scar to mar her beautiful face.

Carter put his hand over hers where it rested on his arm. "I'm happy with the choice I made," he told his grandmother. "Although I can't say that if things had turned out differently, I wouldn't have enjoyed getting a chance to know you," he gallantly said to Fiona.

"It wouldn't have worked out between you and Fiona, anyway," Madelyn said with a sigh.

"Why not?" Desiree asked, her curiosity piqued.

"Fiona has a cat."

Desiree exchanged a look with Carter, and they burst out laughing.

"If you ladies will excuse us, I'd like to dance with my wife," Carter said. "I'm not bad at matchmaking myself," he said with a wink at Madelyn.

Desiree was flustered but pleased by Carter's obvious preference for her company. She was delighted to be dancing with him because it fit into her plans of seduction so well.

A half hour later, Desiree wondered who was seducing whom. She had started by letting her fingers thread into the curls at Carter's nape and gotten all the response she could have hoped for when he drew her closer into his arms. He had let his hand drift down past her waist to the dimpled area above her buttocks and slipped his leg between hers, so she could feel his arousal. It was enough to make her weak in the knees.

His cheek was pressed close to hers—the unblemished one, of course—and his teeth nibbled on her earlobe.

"I've had a wonderful time meeting all your neighbors," he said as he backed away to look at her.

"They like you," she replied.

Desiree was warmed by the desire in Carter's eyes—even though his gaze avoided her scar. She could forgive him that. It wasn't easy to face herself in the mirror each morning, so she knew what it must be like for him. At least there was no obvious distaste apparent on his face when he looked at her.

She mentally pledged to be a good wife to Carter, to trust him, and—after the night was through—to reveal the secret she had kept from him.

"Listen up, everybody!" Faron said. When those gathered for the party were quiet, he said, "It's time to count down the last seconds to the new year. Ten. Nine. Eight."

"Seven. Six. Five," everyone chanted.

Desiree looked into Carter's eyes as she counted with him, "Four. Three. Two."

"One," Carter said. "Happy New Year, Desiree."

"Happy New Year, Carter."

"I think this is where we're supposed to kiss," he said as he looked around the room at the couples caught up in the celebration of the moment.

"I guess it is. Shall we join them?"

Apparently her invitation was the only thing holding Carter back, because he tightened his arms around her and sought out her lips with his. She felt the pressure of his mouth against hers and realized it wasn't enough. Her tongue slipped out and teased the seam of his lips. She felt his smile as he opened his mouth to her. Then she was opening her mouth to him, and the thrust and parry that followed was as erotic a dance as anything Salome might have managed with all her seven veils.

When they broke the kiss at last, they stared, stunned, into each other's eyes.

He was panting.

So was she.

"Let's go home," Carter said. "I'd like to start the new year together—with you in my bed."

Desiree blushed at his forthrightness. But his wishes were very much in accord with her own. "I'll go upstairs and get Nicole."

He put out a hand to stop her. "I asked Maddy if she would keep Nicky overnight. She told me Nicky had stayed with her before, and that she'd be glad to have her."

"But—"

"I told her I'd have to check with you first to make sure it was all right."

Desiree debated only a second before she said, "Tell Maddy I'm thankful for the offer. I'd like to check on Nicole before we go."

"I'll wait down here for you," Carter said.

During the ride home, Desiree chattered like Nicole, talking about how much fun the party had been and how she hoped they could invite some of their neighbors over for supper soon. Carter was silent except for a grunt of assent every so often to let her know he was listening.

Deep down, Desiree harbored the fear that Burley might somehow have already made his way to the Rimrock. So it was with a tremendous sense of relief that she observed when they entered the house that everything appeared untouched. She toed off her fur-lined boots and left them in the pantry along with her coat. Then she stepped into the terry-cloth slippers she had left there when she put on her boots. Carter followed suit, leaving his boots and shearling coat beside hers and heading upstairs in his stocking feet.

"Everything looks exactly as we left it," she said as they passed through the kitchen and into the hall.

Carter gave her a look askance. "You were expecting Santa's elves to come through and change things around?"

Desiree laughed nervously. "Of course not. I just... Never mind."

Carter grasped her hand and started upstairs with her. "Let's go to bed."

There was a wealth of meaning in those words. He stopped upstairs outside her closed bedroom door. "Your room or mine?"

"Yours," Desiree said. Her bedroom held too many awful memories.

Once she arrived at Carter's door she stopped. Even though she had made up her mind to make love to him, she couldn't help feeling afraid.

It was a sign of how attuned Carter was to her in just the little time they had been married that he asked, "Are you sure you want to go through with this?"

"Yes," Desiree said. But the word came out as a hoarse croak. She stared into Carter's eyes, warmed by the glow of desire burning there. In the next instant, he had swept her off her feet and into his arms. She laughed nervously.

"You're safe with me, Desiree," he said as he stepped through the doorway and into his bedroom.

Desiree couldn't have asked for more than that.

Carter had left the lamp burning beside the bed, and it cast the room in shadows. He had already shoved the door closed behind them with his foot, when she realized she had forgotten something. "I wanted to wear my new negligee for you."

Carter grinned. "I'm not saying I don't want to see you in it sometime, but I think it would be wasted tonight."

Desiree stood uncomfortably by the door where he had set her down, as he left her and crossed to the bed to pull down the quilt and sheet. Then he crossed back to stand before her.

"Does this feel as awkward to you as it does to me?" Desiree asked with a shy smile.

"I don't know how you feel," Carter replied, "but this has been the longest three weeks of my life."

Desiree gave a startled laugh. "We've only been married for two."

"I've wanted you since the night I met you, since the moment you came downstairs and I saw you for the first time without that awful moth-eaten coat."

"But my face—"

"Has a terrible scar. I know." He gently removed her hand from where it had crept to cover her cheek. "There's more to you than your face, Desiree. You're a beautiful woman."

But even as he said the words, he was avoiding her scar with his eyes.

Desiree noticed there had been no words of love spoken. But, then, she hadn't expected them. They had met and married under unusual circumstances and had known each other too briefly for stronger feelings to grow between them. The desires of the flesh did not need love or commitment to flourish. The animal instinct to couple and reproduce was bred deep. They could want without loving.

And she did want Carter. Her need grew as his fingertips followed where his eyes led, across the shoulders of her knit dress and lower where the flesh was exposed along her collarbone, then down along the line of buttons between her breasts to her belly, before they fanned out to circle her hips.

"Come here," he murmured as he pulled her toward him. A moment later their bodies were flush from waist to thigh.

Desiree stiffened reflexively at the intimate contact. She closed her eyes, caught her lower lip in her teeth and forced herself to relax. This wasn't Burley. This was Carter. When she opened her eyes, Carter was staring down at her.

Carter realized suddenly how important it was for him to keep a firm grip on his desire. He didn't want to frighten Desiree. And yet he did not feel in control when he was near her. The scent of her, the taste of her, had him hard and ready. He took a deep breath and slowly let it out in an attempt to steady his pounding pulse.

"I can stop anytime you want," he said. "Anytime."

Desiree lifted a disbelieving brow. "Anytime?"

"Anytime. There's no such thing as a point of no return," Carter said. "That's an old wives' tale. A man can stop. It might not be pleasant. But he can stop."

Desiree felt tears welling in her eyes. "I wish—"

"Shh." He put a callused fingertip to her lips. "No looking backward. There's only tonight. Just you and me. I don't want anyone else in this bedroom with us."

She nodded.

He kissed her eyes closed, then let his lips drift downward toward her mouth. Desiree could feel the tension in his back and arms, the raging passion leashed by consideration for her fear. It wasn't fair, Desiree thought, that the man she had loved should have been so brutal, and this stranger so tender.

"Desiree?"

"Don't stop," she whispered.

Slowly, one at a time, he undid the buttons of her navy knit dress. She heard his murmur of approval as he revealed the black lace camisole she had worn, contemplating just such a moment. He slid the dress over her shoulders and freed her arms before shoving it down over her hips until it landed in a circle around her feet. She was left wearing only her camisole and tap pants.

Goose bumps rose on her skin.

"You're cold," he said as he enfolded her in his arms.

"You have on too many clothes," she replied, forcing him away far enough that she could reach the buttons on his shirt. Her hands were trembling, but it wasn't from the cold. Carter smiled and made short work of his buttons, letting the shirt slide down his arms. She pushed his long john shirt up and he pulled it off over his head.

At the sight of his bare chest she paused. He was so different from Burley. There was a small triangle of black curls at the center of his chest and a thin line of black down that headed past his navel. He took her hands and laid them on his chest.

"Touch me, Desiree."

It was easier than she had thought it would be to let her hands roam at will over the firm muscles of his chest. To her amazement, his nipples hardened into peaks as her fingertips brushed across them.

Carter's hands were moving in a mirror image of her own and she felt a corresponding response in her body.

"That feels wonderful," Desiree said breathlessly.

"You can say that again," Carter muttered as Desiree's hands tensed down across his belly. He slid his hands down to cup the warmth between her legs.

"That feels wonderful." Desiree was in a state of euphoria, reveling in the powerful feelings he evoked.

Carter lowered the straps on the camisole. It caught for an instant on the tips of her breasts before slipping to her waist. He shoved it down along with her tap pants.

She immediately crossed her arms over her breasts and belly to cover her nakedness.

He laughed. "What are you hiding?"

She resisted momentarily when he grasped her wrists to remove her hands, but realized she was only postponing the inevitable.

He gasped when he saw what she had been trying to conceal from him. "What the hell?"

His eyes sought hers, asking questions, demanding answers. "I wasn't going to ask how your face got cut," he said in a voice roughened by emotion.

"But I don't think I can keep quiet about the rest of these scars."

She flinched when his hand reached out to the faint, criss-cross scars on her breasts. She hissed in a breath as his fingertips followed the long slash that arced down her belly.

"I was attacked," she said.

"By a man," he concluded. "Which explains why you jump every time I come up behind you. Lord, Desiree, why didn't you tell me?"

She hung her head, knowing she should tell him now about Burley. He had given her the perfect opening to do so. But she couldn't. He would be disgusted with her. And this evening would be at an end. If it wasn't already.

"I know they're ugly to look at," she began.

"Nothing about you is ugly," Carter retorted fiercely.

Not even my face? she wanted to ask. She looked up to find out whether he was telling the truth. His eyes touched her body like hands, searching out her secrets. She kept waiting for his disgust—or her fear—to rise and spoil what was happening between them, but it never came. All she saw in his eyes was admiration, adoration.

"Come to bed, Desiree." Carter took her hand and drew her toward the bed. She knew he could feel her reluctance, because he paused.

"Have you changed your mind?"

She shook her head. "Unless you have."

He shook his head. "Is there something else you need?"

"I want to leave the light on." That would mean he would have to face her scars, but she hoped maybe she wouldn't encounter so many demons of the past if she kept the dark at bay.

He smiled. "That's fine with me."

Carter picked her up again and laid her on the bed, then rid himself of his trousers, long underwear and socks and joined her there. Desiree had already pulled the sheets up to her neck because she felt so self-conscious about her scars.

Carter slipped right under the covers with her and drew her into his arms so their bodies were aligned. They fit as though they were meant to be together, breast and thigh and belly. She could feel his heat and the hardness of his shaft against her thigh.

Her greatest fear was that now that they were in bed together he would satisfy his need and leave her wanting, as Burley had done so often.

She couldn't have been more wrong.

He went back to kissing her, concentrating on her mouth and neck and shoulders until she was undulating beneath him. His hands sought out places on her body she hadn't guessed could be so sensitive, making her arch toward his touch.

But she knew it was taking too long for her to become aroused. She could feel the rigid tension in his shoulders, the hard muscles of his thighs. She knew he was ready. He must be impatient to get it over with.

"I . . . I'm ready now," she told him. She wanted to please him. She wanted him to want to do this again. So she was willing to end her own pleasure so he could find his.

Carter's hand slid down her belly to the nest of curls between her legs. He slid a finger inside, but it didn't penetrate easily.

"I don't think so," he said. "I think maybe you need some more of this." His mouth slid down from her shoulder to her breast, where he circled her nipple with his tongue.

Desiree gasped. "What are you doing?"

"Kissing you."

"There?"

She saw the moment of shock on his face before he asked, "Your husband never kissed your breasts?"

Desiree was totally mortified. Her face turned pink. She shook her head. "No," she breathed. "He . . . he couldn't wait for . . . for the other."

Carter swore under his breath.

She shrank back against the bedding.

"Desiree, honey, I'm not angry with you. Honey, please . . . let me love you."

Desiree eyed him warily. "You . . . you want to kiss my breasts?"

A roguish grin tilted his lips. "Uh-huh."

"It did feel . . . kind of nice," she admitted shyly. She lay back against the pillow, but her whole body was tensed.

"Relax," he crooned. His mouth caught hers in a swift kiss, and while she was still enjoying its effects, he swept lower and captured her nipple with his mouth. He teased, he sucked, he nipped. Desiree felt things she hadn't even imagined were possible.

"I feel . . . I feel . . ."

"What do you feel?" Carter rasped.

"Everything. I can feel *everything!*" Desiree exulted. She wasn't even close to frigid. Far from it. With Carter, her whole body was burning with sensual desire.

Carter's tenderness soon gave way to ardor and became an unquenchable hunger.

"Carter," she begged. "Now!"

Once again, his hand slid down her belly, into the nest of curls, finding another spot she hadn't even been aware existed.

"Oh! Oh, my!" The pleasure was so intense she felt the urge to escape as much as the urge to lie still so he could keep on with whatever it was he was doing. She had done some reading since her divorce from Burley, but words in a book couldn't do justice to what she was experiencing.

"So you think you're ready now," he said in a husky voice.

"Yesss," she hissed.

He pressed a finger inside her, and it slid easily into the moist passage. She recognized the difference between this time and the last, and realized Carter had taken the time to be sure she was aroused.

She knew he had recognized her readiness when he used his knees to spread her legs and placed himself above her. She put her hands at his waist and looked into his eyes.

"It's all right, Desiree. We have all the time in the world."

She clenched her muscles in readiness for the pain she expected. But Carter didn't thrust himself inside her as Burley had. Instead he probed slowly at the entrance to her womb, pushing a little way inside her and then backing off before intruding again. Until finally, without any pain to her—and with a great deal of self-control on his part—he was fully inside her.

It didn't hurt at all! In fact, it felt decidedly good. Her body instinctively arched upward into his.

Carter gave a grunt of pleasure.

Desiree lowered her bottom and thrust again.

Carter groaned.

"Am I hurting you, Carter?"

"You're killing me," Carter said with a husky laugh. "Just please don't stop!"

Desiree was delighted with the reversal of roles, but it wasn't long before Carter was doing his part to help.

With the joining of their bodies, Desiree found herself reaching out to Carter with body and soul, seeking the satisfaction that she had been denied for so long. When it happened, when her body violently convulsed, she tried to fight it.

"Come with me, love. Ride it out. Let it happen," Carter urged.

She looked up and saw the sheen of sweat that beaded his brow, the hank of damp hair that hung over his forehead, the light burning fiercely in his eyes. She could see the leashed passion waiting to erupt, held on a fraying tether. He was keeping his promise to her. Even now, she was in control.

That knowledge freed her to give rein to the passions that threatened to overwhelm her. Her body spasmed, her muscles tightening in exquisite pleasure as a groan forced its way past her throat. Carter thrust once more, arching his head back as he spilled his seed.

The best was yet to come. When they were both sated, instead of abandoning her, Carter reached out to pull her snugly into his arms, with one of his legs thrown over hers in a continuing embrace.

Desiree was breathless, embarrassed and exhilarated all at once. "That was...wonderful," she said with a shaky laugh.

"That word seems to be getting a lot of use tonight," Carter said with chuckle.

"I don't think anything else quite describes how I'm feeling right now," she admitted.

She was afraid to ask him how he felt, but she didn't believe he was dissatisfied, and certainly not disgusted. She didn't want to do anything to spoil the mood. It was hard to believe this sort of ecstasy could be repeated again and again all the years of their married life.

Desiree found solace for her bruised heart in Carter's arms. All the loving, all the gentle care she would have given to Burley, she bestowed on Carter. Tonight held a promise of the future, a hope for the new year. They would be good partners—in bed and out. Unfortunately, the depth of her feelings for Carter were too treacherous to admit or even to acknowledge.

Suddenly Desiree had to escape. The embrace that had felt so comforting now made her feel captive.

"I want to get up," she said in a harsh voice.

Carter was already half-asleep. "What? What's going on?" He was irritable at being woken. "Lie down."

"I'm going back to my own room."

He came fully awake and stared into her eyes. She knew the fear was back, but couldn't explain that this was different from her fear of physical harm. Burley had only beaten and terrified and humiliated her. She had given Carter the power to destroy her heart and soul.

"I need to be alone," she offered by way of explanation.

Carter's lips curled in disgust. "I'm not going to turn into some kind of beast in the middle of the night. But if you want to go, go."

Desiree yanked on a flannel shirt that Carter had left tossed over a ladderback chair and fled the room.

Carter slumped back against the pillow, then smacked it with his fist. All the love he would have given to Jeanine he had bequeathed to the woman he had lain with tonight. The emotions he had experienced as Desiree climaxed beneath him were too dangerous to explore. He hadn't been ready to let her go when she abandoned him. He felt . . . a loss. But what could he have done to stop her? After all, it wasn't as though they were in love. They were only married lovers.

He reached over to turn out the light. He hoped she spent a miserable night alone. He hoped she tossed and turned the way he was sure he would himself. He hoped she had bags under her eyes in the morning the size of suitcases. He hoped—

Desiree screamed. "Carter! Come Quick!"

Carter's blood ran cold at the terror in her voice. A second later he was on his way to her.

Seven

Carter grabbed a pair of jeans, stuck his legs in them and dragged them on as he headed on the run toward Desiree. He found her standing in the doorway to her room, her eyes so wide he could see the whites of them, the back of her hand across her mouth to stifle the awful, tearing sobs that erupted from her throat.

"Desiree, are you all right? Are you hurt? What happened?"

At the sound of his voice she turned and flung herself into his arms, which tightened around her. Over the top of her head he had a view of the chaos in her bedroom.

It had been ransacked. There wasn't an object left upright or unbroken. There were feathers everywhere from the destruction of the pillows, and even her mattress had been slashed. This wasn't the work of a thief. It was the devastation of a psychopath.

"This is crazy," Carter muttered. "Why so much destruction? And why only your bedroom?"

Desiree sobbed harder in his arms. He felt a fierce need to protect her, to crush the fiend who had threatened the woman he held so tightly.

"I'll call the police."

She grabbed him around the neck. "No!"

"Why not? They'll want to investigate. Anybody crazy enough to do something like this belongs in a cage where he can't hurt people. They'll want to find him fast."

Desiree dragged herself free of his embrace. "I know who did this," she said. "But it won't do any good to confront him. He'll just deny everything. Unless I can catch him in the act, they can't do a thing. I have to have evidence," she said bitterly, "before they'll interfere."

Carter felt his stomach turn over. "Who did this, Desiree?"

Her shoulders slumped, and she turned to lean her forehead against the cool wood framing the door. "He said he would come back."

"Who said he would come back?" Carter demanded, his voice laced with the irritation he was feeling at his helplessness.

"Burley Kelton." Desiree turned to look Carter in the eye. "My former husband. I should have told you," she said in an anguished voice. "He's been in prison for attempting to murder me, but he got out today. He warned me he was coming back. I hoped—"

"You hoped that if you had a husband he would keep his distance," Carter said in a voice like a rusty gate.

What a fool he had been! She had used him.

And weren't you using her to get the roots you wanted?

That was different.

How? You both wanted something from each other. So she wasn't totally honest about her motives. Have you been totally honest with her?

The truth was, he had married for his own reasons, not thinking much about hers. The band around his chest loosened enough that he could breathe again.

"Stay here while I check the house to make sure he's gone," Carter said.

Desiree's eyes rounded again in fear. "You don't believe he could still be here, do you?"

"I'm going to find out." Carter ushered her back to his bedroom door. He turned on the light and drew her inside. "Stay here. Close the door behind me and lock it."

Carter had no weapon handy, and wondered what he would do if he encountered the other man armed with a knife. Or a gun.

But the house had an empty feeling. A quiet, thorough search revealed no signs of an intruder. The broken lock on the front door explained how Burley had gotten in.

When Carter returned to his room he knocked and said, "It's me. Let me in."

Desiree stood hesitantly across from him until he opened his arms. Then she flew into them once more.

"Did you find anything?" she asked.

"Nothing. Except a broken lock on the front door."

She gave a shuddering sigh. "Oh, Carter. What am I going to do?"

"You mean, what are *we* going to do? First, we're going to call the police." Before she could protest, he added, "He might have left some fingerprints or some other evidence."

"Do we have to do it now?"

Carter grimaced. "I suppose tomorrow morning is soon enough."

"I'm so sorry I got you involved in all this," she said, her cheek against his chest. "I thought if he knew I was married again, he would leave me alone."

"I guess not," Carter muttered. "So Burley is the one who mistreated you?"

She nodded. She tried to talk but couldn't manage any sound past the knot in her throat.

Carter put an arm around her shoulders and walked over to the bed with her. He sat down with his back against the headboard and pulled her onto his lap. "I want to hear about it," he said.

Desiree realized Carter was almost quivering with fury. But it was all directed at the man who had harmed her.

"I was too young when I married him, and very naive. I . . . I put up with . . . everything . . . as long as I could. While my parents were alive, it wasn't so bad. After they were gone, his abuse got worse.

"That explains all that flinching around me, I suppose."

She nodded, her hair tickling his chin.

"One night after dinner, I got up the courage to ask him for a divorce. He went crazy. He accused me of seeing another man. He told me he'd make sure no other man would want to have anything to do with me. He told me he'd married me 'till death do us part,' and if he couldn't have me no one could.

"We were in the kitchen, and he grabbed a butcher knife. He cut my face first." Her hand protectively covered the scar. "Then he raped me."

"Desiree—"

"Let me finish!" she said. "He laughed while he was carving designs on my breasts. Said he was branding me so any other man I tried to sleep with would know I belonged to him. The wound in the belly came when I told him I would never belong to him, that I was going to leave him if it was the last thing I ever did. He assured me that leaving him would be the end of me.

"If one of the ranch hands hadn't heard my screams and come running, Burley would have killed me. As it was, he escaped the house and ran. Before he left, he promised me he would come back some dark night and finish what he had started. It took six weeks before he was caught. During that time I lived in fear for my life. I left the lights on because I was afraid of the dark. I still am," she admitted in a whisper.

"Desiree—"

"Nine months after he raped me, Nicole was born."

"Oh, my God," Carter said. "Does Burley know about the child?"

Desiree shook her head. "I don't know if he'll figure it out. But he has friends who could tell him I've been living here alone until recently." Desiree's hands snuck up around Carter's neck, where she clung for support. "I've been so afraid he'll do something to hurt Nicole. I know I've been dishonest with you. All I can say is, I'm sorry."

In that instant, Carter was tempted to tell her the truth about himself, that he had also married under false pretenses. But he knew now that his money wasn't what Desiree had been after when she married him. Unfortunately, over the past three weeks he had discovered that he wanted—needed—much more from her than the pleasure to be had from her body.

Telling her the truth would only complicate matters right now.

"He'll be back," Desiree said in a whisper.

"How can you be so sure?"

"I've been through this before," she said. "I was in the hospital for a short while following Burley's attack. After I came home, in the six weeks before Burley was caught, he used to leave signs that he had been around—to terrorize me, I think. Or he would call me on the phone and just breathe. He was always careful not to leave anything that could be used as evidence against him in court."

"The police can question Burley—"

"The police have to catch Burley before they can question him," Desiree said with asperity. "Burley knows this place like the back of his hand, where to hide, all the back roads."

"So you're just going to sit here and wait for him to finish what he's started?" Carter demanded.

"What do you suggest?" Desiree retorted.

"Do you have a gun?"

"No! And I don't intend to get one."

"Then how do you propose to protect yourself?"

There was a pause before she replied, "I was counting on you for that."

There was another pause before he answered, "What, exactly, did you have in mind?"

"There's the chance that your presence here will be enough to deter anything like this from happening again."

"Do you really believe that?"

"I believe Burley will keep his distance so long as you're around." Burley only preyed on things weaker than himself.

"That's going to make it a little difficult for things to get done around here—I mean, if we have to do everything in tandem. And what about Nicole?"

"She would have to be with us, too."

Carter shook his head. "It won't work."

Desire gripped his shoulders. "It could. What other choice do we have?"

Carter tried to come up with some other solution to the problem. But until Burley made a move, there was nothing he could do. "All right," he said. "We'll call the police and report this intrusion tomorrow morning. If they don't find anything—"

"They won't."

"I'll go along with your plan."

She hesitated only an instant before she said, "Thanks, Carter. I won't be a burden, I promise."

Nevertheless, Carter felt a tremendous burden of responsibility. She had put her safety, and Nicole's, in his hands. Once before a woman had asked him to protect her. And he had failed her...and their daughter.

"You can sleep here," Carter said. "I'll be comfortable on the couch."

"Or we could sleep here together," Desiree suggested tentatively.

"You sure?" Carter asked.

"As long as I can have the right side of the bed," she said with a shy smile.

Carter laughed. "Fine."

Desiree settled on her side of the bed as Carter turned out the light. She tossed and turned for several minutes trying to get comfortable. At last, he couldn't stand it any longer. He put an arm around her waist and dragged her back against him, so her bottom spooned into his groin and his knees were tucked behind hers. Her head fit just under his chin, and her flyaway hair tickled his nose.

"Go to sleep," he said gruffly.

He didn't know whether it was because he ordered it or because she was comfortable at last, but the sound of her steady breathing told him sometime later that she was asleep.

Meanwhile, he lay for hours staring into the darkness, confronting the memories he had been running from for six long years.

He had thought himself the happiest of men when he married Jeanine. He was in love, and they had a child on the way. Only years later had he discovered that things were not as they had seemed. By the time Jeanine had come to him with the truth, a tragedy had already been set in motion.

Carter had greeted his wife with surprise and pleasure when she appeared at his forty-third-floor corporate office in downtown Denver. "What are you doing here, Jeanine?"

"We have to talk, Carter."

"I was just going out to lunch," he said. "Join me."

"I think it would be best if we spoke here. In private."

It was then he had noticed the redness around her eyes and the bruise on her cheek, barely hidden by makeup.

He led her over to the black leather sofa in the steel-and-glass office. "Sit down," he said. "Tell me what's going on."

She fidgeted with the gold chain on her purse, refusing to meet his gaze. "I have a confession to make."

Carter's heart was in his throat. There was only one kind of confession a woman made to a man. She was having an affair. He felt a murderous rage toward the unknown man who had seduced his wife.

"I had an affair."

Even though he had been expecting it, hearing the words was like getting punched in the gut. All the air whooshed out of his lungs.

She looked up at him, her gray eyes liquid, as beautiful as she had ever been. "It was while we were engaged."

Furrows appeared on his brow. "That was years ago. Why are you telling me about it now?"

She left her purse on the couch and paced across the plush carpeting. "Because he won't leave me alone!"

Carter rose and followed her to the window overlooking the street below. He actually felt the hairs bristling on his neck when he asked, "Is he the one responsible for that bruise on your cheek?"

She lifted her hand to the revealing mark and winced in pain at even that slight touch. "Yes."

His hands fisted. "I'll take care of it. Tell me where to find him."

"It isn't that simple," she said. The tears began to fall, leaving tracks across her perfect makeup. "You see, he's Alisa's father."

Carter's heart skipped a beat. His face blanched. He couldn't have heard what he had thought he'd heard. "Some other man is the father of my child?"

She nodded.

"Alisa isn't mine?"

"No, she's not."

Carter's stomach churned. His heart was pounding so hard it felt as though he had been running a race. A race he was losing. "Why are you telling me this now?" he asked in a harsh voice.

"Because I need your help," she said. "I realized my affair with Jack—"

"Is that his name?"

"Yes. Jack Taggert. I realized my affair with him was a mistake, but by then I was pregnant. I told him it was over, but he wouldn't take no for an answer. Business took him overseas for five years after you and I were married, but now he's back. He wants to pick up where we left off. And he wants to see Alisa.''

"How the hell does he know Alisa is his?'' Carter demanded.

"She has a birthmark. It's something all the Taggerts have. He saw it, and he knew.''

"Dammit, Jeanine, why the hell didn't you tell me about this *before* we were married?''

"Because I was afraid you wouldn't understand.''

"You're damn right I don't!'' He paced angrily away from her. "Now what?'' he demanded.

"I love you, Carter.''

"Sure you do!'' he said sarcastically. "That's why you've been passing off some other man's kid as mine!''

"Carter, I—''

"I don't want to hear any more of your lies, Jeanine. Just get the hell out of here.''

"Carter, I'm afraid of Jack. He's—''

"He's your problem, not mine,'' Carter said ruthlessly. "You deal with him.''

"You don't understand.''

"I sure as hell don't! Why did you marry me, Jeanine? Why didn't you marry the father of your child?''

"You had more money,'' she snapped back at him.

Carter's lips flattened. "Thanks for that bit of honesty.''

"I was being sarcastic!'' she cried. "I love you, Carter. I need your help. Please!''

He went to the door and held it open for her. "I need to think, Jeanine. Go home."

"You don't seem to understand," she said as she stood on the threshold. "Jack has been stalking me, Carter. He's threatened to kill me if I don't come back to him."

"You expect me to believe that?" he said with a sneer.

"It's the truth."

"I'll call you when I make up my mind what I'm going to do," he said. "Don't let that bastard near Alisa until you hear from me."

He had closed the door quietly behind her, then sunk down along the wall and dropped his head onto his knees. His whole world had been ripped apart. He was furious with his wife for betraying him, hated her for lying to him. It had been a crushing blow to learn that the woman he had loved, and whom he believed had loved him, had really married him because he had more money than the man who had fathered her child.

But most of all, he was devastated by the discovery that his daughter was not his daughter. Alisa, the delight of his life, was not even his own flesh and blood!

Carter thought of the doll he had bought Alisa for Christmas, the one that could talk and drink and wet. Alisa had sat in his lap and played with his tie and told him all about it. He had brushed the blond hair from her eyes and told her she should be sure to write Santa and ask for one. Then he had rushed right out to buy one for her.

Later that fateful day he had asked his secretary to call his wife and tell her he was going on a business trip that would take him out of town for a week. Maybe by the end of that time he could figure out what he was going to do with his life.

But he hadn't been given a week. Three days later, on Christmas Eve, his wife and daughter had been on the way to the Christmas pageant, when they were run off the road in a fiery crash that had completely destroyed both cars. The police had identified the driver of the second vehicle as Jack Taggert.

It wasn't until he heard that his wife and daughter were dead that Carter realized the mistake he had made. Biology wasn't what had made Alisa his daughter. And even if Jeanine had not loved him, he had loved her. As his wife, he had owed her his trust and his protection. He had betrayed her every bit as badly as she had betrayed him. Only he was never going to get the chance to make things right.

Here in Wyoming he had found another daughter who was not his own, another woman who was threatened by a man from her past.

This time he wouldn't fail them.

Carter tightened his hold on Desiree, which was when he realized she wasn't asleep, after all.

"What are you thinking?" she whispered in the dark.

"How did you know I was thinking?"

"You kept making little noises in your throat."

Carter made a little sound in his throat.

"Just like that," she said as she snuggled back into the curve of his hips. "What were you thinking about, Carter?"

"About my wife and daughter." He felt her stiffen.

"About how much you miss them?"

"My wife was being stalked by an old boyfriend when she was killed along with our daughter," Carter said. "She asked me to protect her, but I didn't. I didn't realize how serious the danger was. And we had fought...."

Desiree reached for the light on her side of the bed and turned it on. She saw the pain of his loss etched in his blunt features. She reached out a hand to cradle his bristly cheek. "How awful," she said in a quiet voice. "Why didn't you tell me about this before?"

Carter lifted himself up on his elbow. "It isn't something I'm very proud about. In fact, I've felt guilty about it for years."

"And now you have a chance to atone," Desiree said as she brushed her thumb across his cheek, "by taking care of me and Nicole."

"Something like that," Carter admitted.

Desiree dropped her hand, then reached over and turned out the light. She lay down on the edge of the bed with her back to him and remained very still.

After a few minutes, Carter asked, "What are you thinking, Desiree?"

"How do you know I'm thinking?"

"Because you're so quiet."

At first he thought she wasn't going to answer him. Then she said, "I'm not sure marrying you was the right thing to do."

"Oh?"

"I had hoped that if I was married, Burley would accept the fact that I'm not ever going to let him back into my life. What happened tonight proves that either he hasn't seen you, or he doesn't care. I'm sorry for using you like that, Carter. But I was desperate."

"Why didn't you just sell the Rimrock and go somewhere Burley would never find you?"

"This house was built generations ago by my forebears. Do you understand what I'm saying?"

"Yes. I think so. You have deep roots that tie you to the land." Like the roots he was beginning to grow himself.

"Besides," she said, "if I had run away, Burley would only have followed me. I'd rather stand and fight."

"You didn't do so well the last time you tangled with Burley."

"Last time I didn't have you on my side."

Carter grunted an acknowledgment of her point. Apparently, she thought his presence was going to make a difference. He hoped she was right.

"I'm glad I found you, Carter."

"I'm glad you found me, too. I promise I'll take care of you, Desiree. You and Nicky both."

"Thanks, Carter. I'm kind of tired. I think I'll go to sleep now."

She was curled up on the edge of the bed, as far as she could get from him. He could have left her there. It was clear that after his confession she was having second thoughts about her marriage to him. But Carter didn't want them to start the new year on opposite sides of the bed.

He scooted over to the middle of the bed, reached for Desiree and dragged her back against him.

"Carter—"

"I need you close to me, Desiree."

She lay stiff in his arms a moment longer, then pressed herself close to him. "Happy New Year, Carter."

"Happy New Year, Desiree."

Eight

Desiree knew Carter meant the promise he had made to protect her. But it was depressing to think that the care he took of her over the next weeks and months was motivated by guilt, rather than feelings of love. She wanted more. She wanted him to love her. Because, God help her, she had fallen in love with him. However, she wasn't about to tell him how she felt, because that wasn't part of their bargain. A marriage of convenience shouldn't have emotional strings attached.

Their call to the police on the morning after Burley's rampage through her bedroom had yielded exactly the result Desiree had expected. There were no fingerprints, no solid evidence to connect Burley to the crime. The officers were sorry, they would keep a lookout, but unless they had some proof that Burley was the culprit, there was nothing they could do.

Carter hadn't been satisfied with that. "I'm going to hire a couple of extra hands to help out around here," he said.

"I—we—can't afford it."

"I've seen the books," Carter said. "We can afford it if we cut costs somewhere else. I want some people here, so I'll know you're safe if I'm not around."

"But—"

"No buts."

She had given in. Not graciously. She had argued for a day and a half. But she had seen he was determined, so she had agreed.

Gradually winter had loosened its grip on the land. The buffalo grass and wheatgrass and grama grass had put up sprouts of green. Desiree spent more and more time outside with Nicole, working in her vegetable garden behind the house. She always had one eye on the rolling prairie, waiting for Burley to show up. But he seemed to have disappeared.

Ordinarily she stayed close to the house. But on one unusually warm and beautiful March day, when Nicole was with Carter in the barn, her eyes strayed to the horizon. She caught sight of a patch of colorful wildflowers on the hillside that begged to be picked.

Even though the flowers were within easy calling distance of the house and barn, she debated the wisdom of leaving the area of the house to go pick them. As she dug with her trowel, weeding the carrots and squash and watermelon, she got angrier and angrier over the fact that Burley had made her so much a prisoner that she couldn't even walk a couple of hundred yards to pick wildflowers.

She dropped her trowel, yanked off her gloves and started marching up the hill. She picked wildflowers almost defiantly, breaking the stems and dropping them into her shirt, which she held out like a basket. Once she had picked the patch she had seen from the garden, she whirled to return to the house, which was when she spied another, even more beautiful, patch.

She looked around her, and there was nothing visible in any direction. She wasn't far from the house, still within easy shouting distance.

"He's *not* going to make me a prisoner," she said aloud. She started marching toward the next hill. She did that twice more, and was startled, when she glanced up, to realize she could no longer see the house.

He appeared out of nowhere.

Desiree realized she had been lured into a false sense of security by the extra men Carter had hired, and by the fact Burley hadn't shown his face in the twelve weeks since he had ransacked her bedroom.

"What are you doing here?" she demanded when he rose up to block her way.

"I was just taking a little look around the place. You've made some improvements while I've been away, Ice."

Desiree shuddered at the name he called her. It had hurt when he used it before, because she had believed it was true. Thanks to Carter, the word had lost its power to wound her. If she had ever been like ice in bed, that was no longer true. She lifted her chin and stared into Burley's dark brown eyes.

She wondered what she had found so attractive about him once upon a time. He wore his long hair combed back in front, in an old-fashioned bouffant that reminded her of Elvis. He had gained a bit of weight in prison, so now he was not only tall, but heavyset. A grizzled black stubble coated his cheeks and chin. The twinkling brown eyes that had courted her, that had flirted with lazy winks, were puffy, the color of dull brown mud.

His clothes were dirty and wrinkled, as though he had been sleeping in them. She realized it was entirely possible that he was camped somewhere on the Rimrock.

"You'd better leave," she said. "Or I'll call the police and have you arrested for trespassing."

"Oooh, I'm scared," he said in a singsong voice. "Where did you find the man?"

"What man?"

He grabbed her arms in a grip so tight she knew there would be bruises there tomorrow.

"Don't play games," he snarled.

"His name is Carter Prescott. He's my husband."

"I heard something like that," Burley said. "You can kiss him goodbye. Better yet, kiss me hello."

Desiree kept her teeth clenched as Burley forced a kiss on her. His breath was fetid, and she gagged.

"You've gotten awful high and mighty since I've been gone," he said, angrily shoving her an arm's distance away.

"Carter will kill you," she retorted.

"Not if I kill him first."

Desiree gasped at his threat. "I don't love you anymore, Burley. I don't want to be with you. I want you to leave me alone. And I want you to leave Carter alone."

"What about the kid?"

Desiree's heart missed a beat. "What about her?"

"Who's her father, Desiree?"

"Carter Prescott."

He shook his head. "Uh-uh. Prescott didn't show his face around here till this past Christmas. The kid is what? Five? Six? She's mine, isn't she?"

"No. There was another man—"

"I want to see her," Burley interrupted.

Desiree felt panic clawing at her insides, but she kept her voice calm and firm. "No."

"I'll bet one of those new-fangled blood tests would prove she's mine," Burley said in a silky voice. "Then I could get a court to let me see her, don't you think?"

"Don't do this, Burley. You never wanted children. You told me so every time we—" Desiree cut herself off. She couldn't bring herself to identify intercourse with Burley as making love, not after she had experienced what lovemaking really was.

"I'd be willing to forget about the kid if you paid a little attention to me."

Desiree gritted her teeth to keep the disgust she felt from showing on her face. She should have known Burley was only using Nicole to blackmail her. She was determined not to be a victim again. She decided to promise him anything now. And make sure she was never anywhere he could catch her alone again.

At the sound of approaching hoofbeats, Burley jerked his head around and searched the hillside. "You're expecting company?"

"Carter was planning to join me," Desiree lied.

Burley pulled out a switchblade and snapped it open. "Don't go doing anything stupid," he said. "I'll be back to see you another time. So long, Ice."

Once he was gone, Desiree whirled and ran toward the man approaching on horseback. To her relief, it was Carter. He dismounted on the run, and she met him halfway, sobbing with relief by the time she threw herself into his arms.

"Are you all right?" he asked, clutching her tightly against him.

"I'm fine. I wanted to pick some wildflowers, and I guess I wandered too far and got frightened."

She saw him eyeing the wildflowers strewn carelessly across the ground, flowers she hadn't been holding when they had first spied each other.

"What happened here, Desiree?"

"Nothing."

"Don't tell me that!" Carter said in a harsh voice. "He was here, wasn't he?"

Desiree nodded jerkily. She clung to Carter to keep him from going after Burley. "He has a knife! Let him go."

"How did he get here?"

They heard the roar of a motorcycle, which answered his question.

"I was so scared," Desiree said as she clutched Carter around the waist. "I'm so glad you came. How did you know he was here?"

"I didn't," Carter admitted. "I stepped out of the barn for a minute and looked for you in the garden. When I didn't see you, I thought...I thought maybe something had happened to you." His grip tightened so she could barely breathe. "I don't know what I would do if anything happened to you."

Desiree knew it wasn't love that made him say such things. It was guilt. Carter wouldn't be able to live with himself if he lost another wife to a stalker. Whatever the source, she was grateful for the concern that had sent him hunting for her.

She looked up into Carter's eyes, trusting him enough to let him see her desperation and her fear.

"Burley said he wants to see Nicole. He knows she's his."

"Nicky isn't going anywhere with that man," Carter said. "You don't have to worry about that."

"He is her father."

"Only biologically. I'm Nicky's father now."

Desiree stared up at Carter in surprise. Even though Nicky had been referring to Carter as her daddy for the past three months, it was the first time he had acknowledged himself in that role.

"You want to adopt her?" Desiree asked.

Now it was Carter who looked surprised. "I hadn't thought that far ahead, but I suppose so. Yes."

Desiree laid her head on his shoulder. "Thank you, Carter."

"This time we've got that bastard cold," he said. "He was trespassing on Rimrock land."

"Did you actually see him?"

"No. But I know he was here."

She shook her head, her brown hair whipping her cheeks. "It wouldn't do any good. It's his word against mine."

"Dammit, Desiree! That man should be put away in a cage where he can't hurt you or Nicky."

"I won't go beyond sight of the house again unless someone is with me," she promised. "He won't come near the house as long as there are people around." Her lips twisted ruefully. "He's too smart—and too much of a coward—for that."

"I hate living like this," Carter said.

"And you think I don't?" Desiree responded tartly. "But there's nothing either of us can do about it."

"There's something I can do," Carter said.

Desiree framed his beard-roughened cheeks with her palms and forced him to look at her. "You aren't going to confront him, are you? Because all that would accomplish would be to get one or the other of you killed. I don't want to lose you, Carter. Promise me you'll stay away from him."

His lids dropped to conceal the feral look in his blue eyes. His lashes fanned out like coal crescents across his weathered face. When he opened his eyes again, he had hidden his feelings behind a wall of inscrutability. "I'll stay away from him. But I'm not making any guarantees if he comes back to the Rimrock."

"All right." She let her hands drop to her sides, but kept her eyes on Carter. Now that her fear had dissipated, there was another kind of tension building. She couldn't be around Carter without feeling it. The need. The desire. This time she was the one who let her lids drop to hide her avid expression.

"Desiree?"

Her body trembled at the sound of her name in that husky voice he used when he wanted her. His body almost quivered with animal excitement. The blunt ridge in his jeans was proof of his need. The wind carried with it the musky scent of aroused male.

Desiree lifted her lids and stared up into blue eyes lambent with passion.

It was a sign of how far they had come over the past three months that there was no longer any question whether she was ready for him. She was always as ready for him as he was for her. What was more, she trusted him not to hurt her—no matter how uninhibited their lovemaking became.

So when he grabbed the front of her blouse and jerked, sending buttons flying, she responded by pulling the snaps free on his shirt and forcing it down off his shoulders. His mouth clamped onto her breast and sucked through the lace bra she was wearing. She followed him down onto the soft shoots of new grass, their tangled bodies rolling once or twice until they came to rest with her beneath him.

While he unsnapped her jeans and pulled down the zipper, she did the same to him. He shoved her jeans down, while she released him from his. With a single thrust he was inside her. Carter claimed her as she claimed him, their bodies moving urgently, seeking satisfaction.

"You're mine," Carter said as he climaxed within her.

"Yours," Desiree confirmed. "Only yours."

When it was over, they lay beside each other in the cool grass, staring up into a sky as wide and blue as any on earth.

"Do you ever wonder where you would be now if I hadn't proposed to you in the church parking lot?" Desiree asked.

Carter pulled up some clover and twirled it between his fingers. He leaned over to hold it under Desiree's nose so she could smell the sweet scent. "I'd still be looking, I guess."

"For a wife?"

"For a place to settle down."

"Are you happy, Carter?"

"Are you?" he countered.

Desiree thought about it a moment. "Most of the time."

"And the rest of the time?" She hedged against admitting that what would make her really happy was to know that he loved her. Instead she said, "I don't think we've seen the last of Burley."

"If he comes back, I'll be ready for him."

As the days turned to weeks, and the weeks to a month, Desiree began wishing that Burley would just return so they could get the confrontation over with. The waiting was driving her crazy. Especially since there were signs—ominous things, but nothing she ever dared mention to Carter—that he hadn't gone away.

She found the laundry she had hung on the line in the backyard pulled down into the dirt. The heads of her marigolds were all cut off. A birdhouse was destroyed. And Nicole's Black Angus calf, which had never been sick, not even when it was first born, mysteriously died.

Desiree had been with Nicole when they found the calf. Nicole had let herself into the stall and dropped to her knees beside the calf, which was lying on its side with its tongue hanging out.

"Mommy, what's wrong with Matilda? She isn't moving."

Desiree entered the stall and lowered herself to the hay beside Nicole. "Let's see what the problem is."

She knew the instant she touched the stiff, cold body that the calf was dead. One of the basic laws of farm life was not to make pets of the animals. It was likely they would have to be sold, or killed and eaten. She had broken that rule when she had allowed Nicole to name the calf. Nicole would have to suffer now for her folly.

"Matilda's dead, Nicky," Desiree said.

Her daughter looked up at her in shock, then looked back at the motionless calf. She put a finger on its nose, seeking for breath that wasn't there, and felt the unnatural texture of its skin. Her face scrunched up and tears flowed freely down her cheeks.

Desiree enfolded her daughter in her arms and did her best to console the inconsolable child.

"What happened to him, Mommy? Why did he die?"

Until Nicole mentioned it, Desiree hadn't focused on what might have killed the calf. She looked around her suspiciously. "I don't know. Let's check and see if we can find out what happened."

Having something to do helped both of them. Desiree examined the calf, but there was no obvious wound. Nor was there anything in the feedbox that appeared different or unusual. Desiree did find a white dusting of powder that had sifted through the feed box onto the stall floor.

Poison. Strychnine or arsenic, most likely, she realized.

Which meant that Burley had been there. Desiree was furious that Burley had chosen to kill the calf. She was terrified at the thought that he had been so close, that if Nicole had come in here alone, her innocent daughter might have been confronted by a man fully capable of brutalizing her, perhaps even killing her. Suddenly Desiree no longer felt safe in the barn.

"Come on," she said to Nicole, "let's go tell your daddy what happened."

Grim-lipped, Carter listened to Nicole's tale of woe. He lifted her into his arms and carried her upstairs, where he sat with her until she fell asleep for her afternoon nap.

Desiree waited downstairs for the showdown she knew was coming. Carter didn't keep her waiting long.

"Burley did this." He said it as a fact, or rather, snarled it through his teeth.

"I found some white powder on the floor of the stall that I think might have been poison."

"You don't expect me to keep this from the police, do you?" he asked through tight jaws.

She sighed and lay back in the chair where she was ensconced. "No. I think this should be reported. But I don't think you'll get any satisfaction."

"I want it on the record that someone's been making mischief around here."

"All right."

"You aren't arguing with me."

She sighed again. "It isn't the first time Burley's come onto the Rimrock over the past month."

"What?" He crossed to her and stood with his legs spread and his hands fisted on his hips.

"I didn't want to worry you, but he's done a few things to let me know he's still around."

"Like what?"

"Pulling down the laundry, trampling my flowers, wrecking the birdhouse. Stuff like that."

"And you never said anything to me?"

Desiree could see that Carter was hurt, by the fact that she hadn't shared her problems with him. She shoved herself up out of the chair until she was sitting on the back with her feet on the seat. "There was nothing you could do."

"I could have shared what you were feeling."

"I didn't know you wanted to," she said simply.

"We're husband and wife—"

"Because you wanted the Rimrock," Desiree said, being brutally frank.

She saw him open his mouth to deny it, then snap it shut again. She dropped her head into her hands. "If I'd thought you could help, I would have said something," Desiree admitted. "But there was no way any of those things that happened could be connected with Burley. It would have been a waste of time confronting him."

And dangerous. But she wasn't going to say that to Carter. He was already too anxious to go hunting for Burley Kelton.

Abruptly Carter left the room.

Desiree felt a despair such as she hadn't experienced since the time she was married to Burley and had been bullied by him day and night. She was as much Burley's prisoner now as she had ever been as his wife. And it seemed there was no escape from her nightmare.

She had thought things couldn't get worse, but later that afternoon a police car drove up behind the house. Desiree was on her feet in an instant and running toward it. Carter had been gone all afternoon, and she was deathly afraid that something might have happened to him.

Something had.

When Carter stepped out of the backseat of the police car, Desiree barely recognized him. His face was a mass of cuts and bruises. Both his eyes were black and his lip was swollen. She didn't ask what had happened to him. She knew.

"The doc said to keep some ice on those bruises, Mizz Prescott," the young patrolman said. He turned to Carter and grinned. "That's some right cross you've got. Never saw a man go down so hard as Burley did."

Desiree stared in vexation as Carter tried to return the grin. His face was too battered to manage it.

"When you two are through exchanging compliments I'd like to follow the doctor's orders and put some ice on Carter's face," she said in a frigid voice.

The patrolman tipped his hat. "Sure, Mizz Prescott. The judge'll be expecting you on Monday," he reminded Carter.

Desiree didn't wait to see if Carter followed her. She marched into the kitchen and began pulling ice from the freezer and wrapping it in a dish towel. When she turned, he was standing in the doorway.

"Sit down and shut the door," she snapped.

"He looks worse than I do," Carter said as he dropped with a groan into a kitchen chair.

"That's comforting," Desiree said sarcastically.

"It had to be done."

"I don't know why men think everything can be settled with violence. What have you accomplished except to give Burley another reason to want revenge?"

"He won't be doing anything anytime soon," Carter said with satisfaction.

"Are you going to end up spending time in jail because of this?" Desiree asked with asperity.

Carter started to grin again, put a hand to his puffy lip and thought better of it. "You may not believe this, but Burley started it. I was only defending myself."

"Where did you find him?" Desiree asked.

"There's a bar in Casper where he hangs out."

"Where's Burley now?"

"In jail. Or the hospital."

"Oh, Carter," Desiree said as she eyed his battered face. "You foolish, foolish man. You didn't have to do this for me."

His features hardened, his eyes narrowed. "I didn't do it for you," he said. "I did it for Nicky."

Desiree turned away so he wouldn't see how hurt she was. Carter didn't—couldn't—love her, but he had given his affection to her daughter. She tried to be happy that Nicky had found such a protector. It was hard not to wish that he could love her just a little bit, too.

"Desiree?"

Carter took her hand and pulled her onto his lap. She laid her head on his shoulder and felt him stroking her back, playing with her hair.

"I have a confession to make," he said in a quiet voice.

"What?"

"I've wanted to get my hands on Burley Kelton ever since I first realized he was responsible for the scar on your face." He paused and added. "What he did to the calf...it was just an excuse to go after him."

Desiree let her hands slip into the hair at Carter's nape. "You foolish, foolish man," she whispered. "I'd rather have a hundred scars than see one bruise on this face of yours."

Carter's arms tightened around her. They sat there for a long time. Wishing things were different.

She wished that he loved her.

He wished that she could love him.

Neither spoke their wishes, both being too grown up to believe that dreams do come true.

Nine

As spring passed into summer, Burley kept his distance. Maybe Carter had beat some sense into him after all, Desiree mused. She began to hope that perhaps Burley had changed his mind about wanting her, that he had gotten over his unhealthy obsession. Maybe he had found someone else and that was why she hadn't seen hide nor hair of him—or any sign that he had been watching her. She began to relax her vigil, to make occasional forays from the house on her own.

Carter was not so sanguine about Burley's intentions. When he caught Desiree hunting for four-leaf clovers up in the hills behind the house one afternoon during Nicole's nap, he lashed into her. "Are you crazy?" he demanded. "Or do you have a death wish?"

"What's the matter with you?" Desiree demanded, her fists perched on her hips.

"I happen to care what happens to you," he retorted.

His comment smacked too much of the guilt she knew he felt, and not enough of the love she wished for in vain. "Don't worry," she snapped back at him. "I won't get myself murdered by a stalker. Lord knows how you would survive it a second time!"

His face bleached white and his mouth flattened into a thin line. "If you don't care whether you live or die, I don't suppose it makes much difference what I think."

Desiree was still too angry to be sorry for the wound she had inflicted on Carter. She had flung the accusation at him hoping he would deny that guilt was what motivated his care for her, hoping he would contradict her with protestations of love. Instead he had responded to her wound with a wound of his own.

"Faron has a bull I want to take a look at," Carter said through clenched teeth. "I was going to ask you to come with me, but I can see you've got other plans." He turned and marched down the hill.

She watched him speak to one of the men he had hired to watch over her. The two appeared to argue for a moment before Carter got into his pickup and gunned the engine, raising a cloud of dust as he peeled out of the backyard.

Desiree sank down onto her haunches and dropped her head on her knees. How could she expect Carter to mention love, when she was so careful not to speak the word herself? She couldn't go on this way. When Carter returned, she was going to have to tell him how she really felt. The mere fact he didn't love her back wasn't going to change anything.

Desiree wasn't aware how long she had been sitting there, until she realized she wasn't alone anymore.

"Carter?"

"Guess again."

A shiver of terror raced down Desiree's spine. She lurched to her feet and started to run. She didn't get far before Burley caught the tails of her shirt and hauled her to a stop.

She turned and fought him like a wildcat, her nails raking his face, her fists beating at him. She screamed, knowing there was help not far away.

"Don't waste your breath," Burley said with a laugh. "The man your husband left to watch over you drove away five minutes ago."

Desiree paused to stare in horror at Burley's malicious smile of triumph. "If you touch a hair on my head Carter will hunt you down," she threatened.

"Carter will be dead before you are," Burley retorted. "Come on." He began hauling her down the hill toward the house.

"Where are we going?"

"I want to see my kid," Burley said.

"No," Desiree begged. "Please, do whatever you want with me, but leave Nicky alone."

He ignored her, tightening his hold and yanking her after him.

Desiree kicked at him and caught him behind the knee, causing his leg to buckle. Instead of losing his hold, he dragged her down with him. Burley was good and angry by the time he got back on his feet. He slapped her once, hard enough to split her lip and make it bleed.

"Don't do that again, Ice," he warned. "Or I might have to get mean."

Desiree dug in her heels as Burley dragged her down the hill. She had no doubt of the fate that awaited her when they reached the house. What terrified her was the thought of what Burley might do to Nicole. She had to find some way to escape him, or to render him helpless. Carter was gone. She would have to protect Nicole herself.

Think, Desiree! Think!

By the time they reached the kitchen door, Desiree still had no idea how she was going to save herself and her daughter. By the time they reached the foot of the stairs, she was frantic.

Think, Desiree, think!

But her wits had been scattered by terror. No plan of action came to mind.

Fight, Desiree. Don't give up without a fight.

But he was so much stronger! If only words could kill, she thought. She knew they could wound. She had hurt Carter easily enough.

Words. Use words against Burley!

They had reached the top of the stairs and were heading down the hall to Nicole's room.

"You really ought to stop calling me Ice, you know," Desiree blurted.

"If the shoe fits," Burley said with a sneering glance.

"But it doesn't," she protested. "It wasn't me who had the problem in bed, Burley. It was you."

He stopped so abruptly she ran into his back. He whirled around to face her. "Who says?"

"I'm not cold in bed with Carter," she taunted. "I'm hot. Steamy. He's a better lover than you could ever think of being."

"We'll just see about that," Burley said.

Desiree had accomplished her purpose. Burley was no longer headed for Nicole's room. He was dragging her back down the hall in the other direction, toward her bedroom. She didn't want to imagine what was going to happen when they got there.

As they crossed the threshold into her bedroom, Desiree was very much afraid she might have jumped right from the frying pan into the fire. She only knew that she had to stay alive. For Carter's sake.

What on earth was she going to do now?

Carter was furious with Desiree and even angrier with himself. Why hadn't he just told her he was in love with her? So what if she hadn't even mentioned the word? So what if she had married him just to have someone to protect her from Burley Kelton? The fact he loved her wasn't going to change, even if she didn't love him back.

He wished he could be sure that hired man wouldn't take off before he got back. He had promised Jubal Friar that he could have the afternoon off, but that was when he thought he was going to have Desiree and Nicole with him. Jubal had been upset that Carter had gone back on the agreement. Carter had threatened that if Jubal didn't stay, he was fired.

He hadn't waited for an answer from Jubal before he had jumped into his pickup and taken off. What if Jubal had just walked away? That would mean Desiree and Nicole were alone on the Rimrock right now. Burley would find no one to say nay if he decided to go after the two people who meant everything to Carter.

Carter turned the wheel of the truck so sharply that it skidded as he made the U-turn to take him back to the Rimrock. He knew he was going to feel like a tomfool when he got back and found everything just as he had left it. But a gnawing in his gut told him he would be forever sorry if he didn't make sure.

His heart leaped to his throat when he drove up behind the house and realized Jubal's truck was gone.

"Damn him! And damn me for a stubborn fool!" he railed to himself.

He looked up on the hillside, but there was no sign of Desiree where he had left her. He checked the garden, but she wasn't there. He gave the barn a glance, but realized it was far more likely she was in the house. It wasn't long before Nicole would be up from her nap.

He entered the house quietly, listening for the voice of his wife, the laughter of his daughter. Everything was deathly silent. He was on the stairs when he heard the murmur of voices. A woman's. And a man's. Burley Kelton was upstairs! Judging from the sound, he was in Desiree's bedroom. And Desiree was in there with him.

Carter felt the contradictory urges to race up the stairs and to remain as silent as a shadow. He couldn't do both. He opted for silence. If he could surprise Burley, the situation might be resolved with a minimum of bloodshed. Not that he minded shedding Burley's blood. But he didn't want to see Desiree hurt. Not before he told her he loved her. Not before they had a chance to explore their feelings for each other.

He bit his lip to remain silent when he heard Desiree taunting Burley about his prowess as a man. Did the fool woman think she was invincible? By the time she was through pricking Burley's pride, the ex-convict was going to attack her like the maniac he was.

He could hear the snaps coming undone on Burley's shirt, the rasp of his zipper and the rustle of cloth as his jeans came off. One more second, another second and the man would be naked and vulnerable. Then Carter would attack.

It didn't take another second before he heard a scuffle in Desiree's room.

"Give me my knife, you bitch!" Burley shouted. "If I have to take it from you, I'll break your arm."

Carter's heart shot to his throat as he charged into the bedroom. When the door crashed open, he saw that Burley was still dressed in his long johns. The huge man wrenched the knife from Desiree's fist and backhanded her, sending her flying against the wall.

Carter saw red. "How would you like to try that on someone your own size?" he said with a low growl of menace.

Burley ignored Desiree and turned to face this new foe. "Well, well, well. If it isn't the husband. Desiree and I were just renewing our acquaintance, so to speak." He waved the knife in front of him. "Come on in and join the fun."

With his eyes, Carter warned Desiree to stay put. Then he gestured Burley forward with his hands. "Come on, big man. Let's finish this once and for all."

"Fine by me," Burley said.

Carter had taken a step toward Burley when he heard a small noise behind him. At the same instant he turned to investigate, Desiree screamed, "Nicole, call 911!" and Burley charged.

The little girl turned and fled downstairs.

"Carter!" Desiree cried. "Look out!"

Carter arched his body, so the knife that would have cut him deep merely left a bloody arc across his chest.

"I'm going to kill you," Burley said.

Carter said nothing, merely watched his adversary with intent blue eyes, waiting for the next attack, looking for any chance to get in under Burley's guard.

Both men had forgotten about Desiree, who hadn't been idle. The only thing she had found to use as a weapon was an antique pitcher and bowl that sat on her chest. She grabbed the pitcher and swung it at Burley.

Because he was so tall, the pitcher's effect was lessened. Instead of being knocked out by the blow, Burley was merely irritated and distracted by it.

Desiree's distraction was exactly what Carter had been waiting for. He shot forward and grabbed the wrist that held the knife and began applying pressure to make Burley release it.

Unfortunately, Desiree hadn't retreated quickly enough after hitting Burley, and he managed to grasp her hair and pull her toward him. When she was close enough, he caught her head in the crook of his other arm.

Burley smiled a feral grin and turned to Carter. "Let go of my wrist, or I'll crush her head like a walnut."

"Don't do it," Desiree said. "He'll only kill you, too, before he kills me."

Carter wavered, uncertain what he should do.

Desiree saw that Carter would let Burley kill him rather than watch her be killed before his eyes. She did the only thing she could think of to do.

She pretended to faint.

Unready for so much deadweight, Burley watched in dismay as Desiree slid through his arm and onto the floor at his feet. He tried to take a step forward, but stumbled over her. As he fell, the knife the two men had been struggling over imbedded itself deep in his chest.

Carter waited a moment to see whether the big man would get up. But the knife had done its work.

Carter went down on one knee and pulled Desiree into his arms. "Desiree? Darling, are you all right? Are you hurt? Please say something!"

"I...I..." Three simple words, *I love you,* and she didn't have the courage to say them. Desiree slowly opened her eyes and beheld the worried, beloved face hovering over her.

"What is it you're trying to say, darling?"

"Oh, Carter, I...I...I'm glad you're all right."

He kissed her. A deep, possessive kiss, that claimed and captivated her. Then he lifted her into his arms, stepped over Burley and turned to pull the door closed behind him.

The sound of sirens in the distance announced that help was on the way. And reminded Desiree of her daughter. She struggled to be set down. Once on her feet, she clambered down the stairs, with Carter right behind her.

"Nicky? Where are you?"

She found her daughter sitting at the kitchen table, with the phone at her ear, still talking to the 911 operator. "I have a mommy and a daddy," she was saying, "just like my friend Shirley."

Desiree picked up her daughter and hugged her tight, while Carter took the phone and explained to the operator that the situation was under control. When he hung up the phone he turned to embrace his wife and daughter.

"Who was that mean man, Mommy? Why did he want to hurt Daddy?"

Desiree met Carter's eyes and begged him for an explanation that a five-year-old could understand.

"He was just a man who got lost and scared," Carter said.

"Where is he now?" Nicole asked.

"He's in your mother's room. He had an accident."

"Is he all right?"

Carter reached out a hand to smooth Nicole's bangs from her eyes. "No, Nicky. He's dead."

"Oh. Can we still go see Maddy this afternoon?"

Carter and Desiree exchanged a look that expressed their gratefulness that Nicole was too young to understand the horror of what had happened.

"Maybe we'll have time to go see Maddy after the police are gone," Carter replied.

But it was well after dark before the police had finished their investigation, collected Burley's body and warned Carter not to leave the neighborhood. Desiree's room was cordoned off, and she had instructions to stay out of it until the police had another chance to look around in the morning.

Desiree had retreated to the kitchen and prepared a meal that she was loath to eat. She pushed the food around her plate, washed the dishes after dinner, then headed upstairs to bathe Nicole and put her to bed. She couldn't help shuddering as she passed the closed door to her bedroom.

It was over. The years of horror, of dread, were finished at last. She was free.

Carter joined her at Nicole's bedside and put his arm around her as she read her daughter a story from the book Nicole had given Carter for Christmas. It had only been a few short months, but it felt as though she had known the man sitting beside her for a lifetime.

When the story was done, Carter leaned over and kissed Nicole on the forehead. She threw her arms around him and hugged him. "I love you, Daddy," she said.

Desiree saw the moistness in Carter's eyes, and fought to keep from crying herself.

"I love you, too, Nicky," he said.

Abruptly Desiree rose and left the room, heading for the deep, comfortable chair in the parlor. She sank into it wearily and waited. It wasn't long before Carter joined her.

"We have to talk," she said as he sat down on the sofa across from her.

"Yes, we do," Carter agreed.

"The reason I married you no longer exists," she said tentatively. "As for the reasons you married me—"

"I married you to have a place where I belong. That holds as true now as it did the day we married."

Desiree felt her heart sink to her toes. She had known he only wanted roots. She had confirmation of it now. She couldn't bear staying married to him, when all he really wanted was the ranch. "Now that I'm no longer in danger, there's no reason for us to stay married. We could just be business partners," she suggested.

"Is that so?"

Carter realized that he had to reach for happiness with both hands, or he was going to lose it. "There are a few things you might like to know before we change things around here," he said.

Desiree cocked her head. "Such as?"

"I've found everything I've been searching for my whole life right here on the Rimrock," he said.

"You mean you've put down roots."

"Yes, I have. Only what I've discovered is that roots aren't a particular place or a thing that can be bought. All the money in the world—" He paused and flushed before he continued. "And I have quite a bit—won't buy roots."

"You're rich?"

He ignored her and went on, "Roots are a sense of belonging. Roots grow wherever the people you love are. This is where you are, Desiree. And Nicky. I could never give you up now."

Desiree lifted her eyes to meet Carter's intense gaze. She discovered that he was looking right back at her, and that his loving gaze didn't avoid the scar on her cheek, but encompassed it. She suddenly realized that her terrible scar no longer existed for him, except as a beloved part of her. Desiree launched herself from the chair into Carter's open arms.

"I love you, Carter. I have for so long!"

"I love you, too, Desiree, but I was too damned scared to admit it."

They headed upstairs together, smiling. Actually, they were grinning like idiots. Once in Carter's bedroom, they undressed each other slowly and carefully. His lips found the teardrops of joy at the corners of her eyes and followed them down her scarred cheek to her mouth, where his tongue joined hers in a passionate exchange.

They spent the night loving each other, reveling in the knowledge that their lovemaking was an extension of the feelings they had for each other. They were still twined in each other's arms the next morning—like the gnarled roots of a very old oak—when Nicole joined them there.

She climbed under the covers and stuck her feet on Desiree's thigh, only it turned out to be Carter's, instead.

Carter yelped. "How can your feet be so cold in the middle of summer?" He grabbed for them to warm them with his hands.

Nicole giggled as she snuggled down under the covers. "My friend Shirley has a sister," she said. "Do you think if I asked Santa, he would bring me a sister for Christmas?"

Carter chuckled.

Desiree laughed.

"It is entirely possible," Carter said.

"Entirely," Desiree agreed with a knowing smile.

Birds sang outside the window as the sun rose on a new day. They were a family, Carter thought, with roots and branches and little buds. It was a great beginning for a solid family tree.

* * * * *

Take 4 bestselling love stories FREE

Plus get a FREE surprise gift!

Special Limited-time Offer

Mail to Silhouette Reader Service™

P.O. Box 609
Fort Erie, Ontario
L2A 5X3

YES! Please send me 4 free Silhouette Desire® novels and my free surprise gift. Then send me 6 brand-new novels every month, which I will receive months before they appear in bookstores. Bill me at the low price of $2.49 each plus 25¢ delivery and GST*. That's the complete price and—compared to the cover prices of $2.99 each—quite a bargain! I understand that accepting the books and gift places me under no obligation ever to buy any books. I can always return a shipment and cancel at any time. Even if I never buy another book from Silhouette, the 4 free books and the surprise gift are mine to keep forever.

326 BPA AJJ3

Name	(PLEASE PRINT)	
Address		Apt. No.
City	Province	Postal Code

This offer is limited to one order per household and not valid to present Silhouette Desire® subscribers. *Terms and prices are subject to change without notice. Canadian residents will be charged applicable provincial taxes and GST.

CDES-94R   ©1990 Harlequin Enterprises Limited

SILHOUETTE *Desire*

COMING NEXT MONTH

#847 BEWITCHED—Jennifer Greene
Jock's Boys series
April's *Man of the Month*, Zach Connor, swore off family life long
ago. But could he resist single mom Kirstin Grams and a matchmaking
ghost who was intent on setting the two up?

#848 I'M GONNA GET YOU—Lass Small
Fabulous Brown Brothers
Tom Brown wanted Susan Lee McCrae, a honey-blond beauty
with a streak of Texas stubbornness and a string of admirers. But he
didn't want her just for now...he wanted her for always!

#849 MYSTERY LADY—Jackie Merritt
Saxon Brothers series
Sexy Rush Saxon was searching for riches, but found a floundering
construction business and the last demure woman on earth. But
Valentine LeClair held a secret she would never share with
this ex-playboy.

#850 THE BRAINY BEAUTY—Suzanne Simms
Hazards, Inc. series
Egyptologist Samantha Wainwright had no time for an ex-Boy Scout
doing a good deed. But for Jonathan Hazard, it wasn't just his job to
protect this beauty...it was also his pleasure!

#851 RAFFERTY'S ANGEL—Caroline Cross
Years ago ex-agent Chase Rafferty had killed an innocent man. Now
why was beautiful Maggie McKenna, the victim's wife, helping Chase
get on with *his* life?

#852 STEALING SAVANNAH—Donna Carlisle
C.J. Cassidy needed to prove that he, was no longer a thief.
But how could he when all he could think about was stealing
Savannah Monterey's heart?

As seen on TV!
Free Gift Offer

With a Free Gift proof-of-purchase from any Silhouette® book,
you can receive a beautiful cubic zirconia pendant.

This gorgeous marquise-shaped stone is a genuine cubic
zirconia—accented by an 18" gold tone necklace.

(Approximate retail value $19.95)

Send for yours today...
compliments of 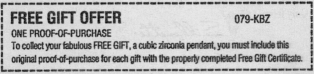 *Silhouette®*

To receive your free gift, a cubic zirconia pendant, send us one original proof-of-
purchase, photocopies not accepted, from the back of any Silhouette Romance™,
Silhouette Desire®, Silhouette Special Edition®, Silhouette Intimate Moments® or
Silhouette Shadows™ title for January, February or March 1994 at your favorite retail
outlet, together with the Free Gift Certificate, plus a check or money order for $2.50
(do not send cash) to cover postage and handling, payable to Silhouette Free Gift Offer.
We will send you the specified gift. Allow 6 to 8 weeks for delivery. Offer good until
March 31st, 1994 or while quantities last. Offer valid in the U.S. and Canada only.

Free Gift Certificate

Name: _____

Address: _____

City: _____ State/Province: _____ Zip/Postal Code: _____

Mail this certificate, one proof-of-purchase and a check or money order for postage
and handling to: SILHOUETTE FREE GIFT OFFER 1994. In the U.S.: 3010 Walden
Avenue, P.O. Box 9057, Buffalo NY 14269-9057. In Canada: P.O. Box 622, Fort Erie,
Ontario L2Z 5X3

FREE GIFT OFFER   079-KBZ
ONE PROOF-OF-PURCHASE
To collect your fabulous FREE GIFT, a cubic zirconia pendant, you must include this
original proof-of-purchase for each gift with the properly completed Free Gift Certificate.

079-KBZ